I0676014

Scott Sherwood

The Washington Decree

"The Constitution is the guide which I never will abandon."

G. Washington

This book is a work of fiction. Names, characters, businesses, organizations, places, events, and incidents either are a product of the author's imagination or used fictitiously. Any resemblance to actual persons, living or dead, events, or locales is entirely coincidental.

Copyright © 2025 by Scott Sherwood

All rights reserved.

eBook ISBN: 979-8-9941934-0-2

Paperback ISBN: 979-8-9941934-1-9

To my wife Karen

For your unconditional love and support

Table of Contents

Key Characters

President of the United States – Ted Hawley – 68. A Harvard-educated autocratic populist who came up through the Machiavellian Texas political system. He's the grandson of one of Texas's original oil tycoons and grew up surrounded by enormous wealth despite his attempts to appear as a self-made "man of the people." Despite his enormous family wealth, Hawley is personally nearly broke after both a series of expensive divorces and losing a fortune in fracking when oil prices collapsed a few years ago. To keep his companies afloat, he had to turn to outside private investment after all the major banks refused to continue doing business with him. Where this money came from has never been disclosed.

Vice President - Joe Harris – 57. Plucked from obscurity by Hawley to be his running mate. Former President of a small religious college in Oklahoma. Married but has had numerous affairs that Hawley has proof of.

Speaker of the House - Michael McCollins – 59. A career politician. Started off as a moderate and has moved to the right. Will do what it takes to remain in power. Owes his speakership to Hawley.

Chairman of the Joint Chiefs of Staff - James Bragg – 63. Promoted to Chairman by Hawley over several more senior officers. Early in his career he was implicated in a civilian massacre by troops under his command in the Middle East. Was found not to be at fault (but Hawley has evidence he gave unofficial/verbal approval for the attack).

Attorney General - Mark Clark – 48. Former Attorney General of Texas. Prior was in private practice and was Hawley's family attorney. Knows where Hawley has buried the bodies and has been lavishly paid to keep the secrets.

All four know that Hawley possesses information that will destroy their careers and families.

Senate Majority Leader: John Webster – 57. Defeated for his party's Presidential nomination by Hawley in 2032. Last mainstream Conservative to hold a position of power. He and Hawley despise each other.

Secret Service Agent: Jimmy Walsh – 27. Former US Navy Seal, ex-boyfriend of Elle Rockefeller.

Chief Justice United States Supreme Court: Anthony Hoyt – 65. Former Professor at Yale Law School. A traditionalist who has staunchly defended the power of the Supreme Court since he assumed the Chief Justice role 20 years ago.

Associate Supreme Court Justice: Ginny Coney – 52. Appointed to the bench by Hawley. Considered a hardcore conservative and a member of Opus Dei.

Associate Supreme Court Justice: Samuel Bomgardner – 69. Appointed to the bench by Hawley. Former Chief Justice of the Mississippi Supreme Court. His brother is a former business partner of Hawley's.

President-elect: Tracy Rockefeller – 53. Born and raised in Virginia. Dartmouth-educated. Former banker who went into politics. Two-term conservative governor of New York before switching parties after the rise of the Tea Party movement. Was married briefly to James Rockefeller. Divorced when he came out as gay but has remained close and enjoys the support of the broader Rockefeller family. One child, Elle who she is very close to.

Daughter of the President-elect: Elle Rockefeller – 25. Studying for her PhD in Economics at Princeton. Served on her mother's campaign. Brilliant and an accomplished athlete.

Vice President-elect: Chris Bolton – 49. Born and raised in San Francisco. Career politician and member of the House of Representatives for 10 terms before becoming the VP nominee. One of the more liberal and outspoken members of the house. Was nominated as VP to shore up support for the ticket on the left of the party. Highly ambitious and ruthless with known Presidential aspirations.

George Post – 54. New York Real Estate Scion; Dartmouth Classmate of Tracy Rockefeller and Susan Lewis.

The members of the 13 are:

Virginia: Bill McLean – 65. The Governor of Virginia, close ally and mentor to Senate Majority Leader John Webster.

Delaware: Kathy Curtis- 48. Currently the Governor of Illinois.

Rhode Island: John Teruel – 68. Former CEO of Lockheed Martin, Defense industry insider of insiders.

Connecticut: Harry Bell – 58. The CEO Bank of Manhattan and first among equals in the 13.

Pennsylvania: Charles Taylor – 60. US Army General in charge of the United States Northern Command. West Point Graduate. Highly decorated and hugely respected career military officer. Should have been appointed Chairman of the Joint Chiefs of Staff in the last round but passed over by Hawley in favor of General James Bragg.

Massachusetts: Walter Lockwood – 50. Supreme Court Associate Justice, close ally of Anthony Hoyt. Was a student of Hoyt's at Yale.

New Hampshire: Susan Lewis – 53. Senator from New Hampshire, went to Dartmouth with Tracy Rockefeller and has remained close. Encouraged her to run for President and was a major supporter of her campaign.

Georgia: Lynn Tyler – 55. Former Mayor of Atlanta, great-grandparents were freed slaves.

New York: Nate Burr – 56. Managing Partner of Burr & Watson, one of New York's most prestigious Law Firms. Distant cousin of Walter Lockwood.

New Jersey: Julia Jackson – 45. Newscaster; Anchor on the CBS Evening News.

Maryland: Sam Fitzwilliams – 52. Former NFL Quarterback. Won 2 Super Bowls with the NY Giants. Retired early before injuries took their toll. Currently a highly regarded Republican Congressman from Illinois. Graduated from Northwestern.

North Carolina: George Damon – 42. A-list Hollywood Actor, married an English Princess.

South Carolina: Jennifer Remington – 43. Professor, University of Chicago Booth Business School.

The Rules of the 13:

They are sworn to protect the US Constitution at all costs, remove those that threaten it, and then return power to the people's representatives as quickly as possible.

Each member of the 13 is chosen by his/her predecessor. The appointment is for life. A member of the 13 can only be removed from the group for treason and it requires a vote of 10 of the 13 members.

The 13 are led by the "1st among equals". They are appointed for a four year term by a simple majority vote and is the Chief Justice of the Supreme Court's primary point of contact.

Upon becoming a member of the 13, you need to identify your successor and place that person's name in a sealed envelope which is given to the "1st among equals". Should you die suddenly, that individual will be approached to take your place.

Traditionally the 13 have only met officially once every 4 years after the US President has been sworn in for a new term. At these meetings they have toasted to President Washington and the successful continuation of the great US experiment.

The 13 Guarantors (within the walls of the 13's chambers, when formality is demanded, they refer to each other not by name, but by the states their seat originally represented):

Each of the original 13 was a US Senator, hand-picked by Washington. He did not necessarily select individuals he liked but did so based on merit, contributions to American Independence, and family roots in the young nation. For Washington, it was critical that every man chosen was deeply committed to both democracy and the "Great American Experiment". While the original 13 were all white males, over the years, the 13 evolved like the nation and became a melting pot of different races and cultural backgrounds.

Prologue
1794 - Mount Vernon

Candlelight licked the edges of a map. Snow worried at the windows; a wind combed the black branches outside. George Washington sat with his jaw set in a way that convinced portraits to paint him heroic. Across from him, John Jay's fingers were ink-stained and deft.

"Your Majesty," Washington said, making a face as if he'd bitten a lemon. "A foolish suggestion."

"A provocative one," Jay answered dryly. "Meant, I suspect, to test how close to a crown your head would lean."

Washington looked down at the parchment between them. Not a law. More powerful at its core. A decree, from the father of our nation and signed not just by his friends, colleagues, and rivals, but all fellow founders—a silent hope in the face of unknown but anticipated future emergencies. Washington knew and understood men, which is what made this necessary.

"Hamilton's lifetime presidency," Washington said. "Adams's taste for majesty. And now factions harden into parties." He exhaled. "We need a device that supersedes all factions."

"We entrust it to the Chief Justice," Jay said. "And to thirteen Americans whose allegiance is not to men, but to our great experiment—drawn from the original states, the senior senators already proven."

"And we bury it under the obvious, where no one will see," Washington murmured.

Jay nodded. "We will sign it—and we will have the governors, the President Pro Tempore, the Speaker, the Court—and finally you—sign it, so that it rests with permanent authority, more powerful in fact than any amendment."

Washington pressed his seal into wax. When he lifted it, the imprint of his decision glowed.

"For the times," he said, "when the people need to be reminded that they are sovereign."

Day 1 - Wheels in Motion

Election Day –Oval Office - Washington D.C.

The Oval Office glowed with television blue. Maps of the United States crawled with red and blue counties, edges bleeding. The grandfather clock ticked as if measuring out the republic in inches.

Hawley stood in shirtsleeves, tie loosened, watching the numbers fall the wrong way. Around him, his trusted circle moved like anxious fish: Attorney General Mark Clark with his polished smile and dead eyes; Vice President Joe Harris feigning prayerful calm; Chairman of the Joint Chiefs James Bragg, massive and impassive in a dark suit; the Speaker of the House, Michael McCollins, eager, sweaty; a handful of comms aides, legislative whisperers, and the loyal lawyers who wrote executable lies.

"Turn off the noise," Hawley said. Someone muted the televisions. The room exhaled.

"Sir," Clark said, "the exit polls do not look good. Rockefeller is polling ahead of us in Pennsylvania, Michigan, Wisconsin, and Ohio."

"Shut up." Hawley didn't look at him. He looked at Bragg. "General. Remind me about order."

Bragg's face didn't change. "Order is maintained by lawful command," he said. "And by clarity of intent."

"Clarity," Hawley repeated, tasting the word like a coin. He turned then, letting his gaze tick across them, one by one. He knew exactly what each man owed him. Harris's hotel room receipts. McCollins's quiet PAC money. Bragg's deniable assent to a massacre in a valley no one could pronounce. Clark's signatures on paper that should have burned.

All of them had come up through the same funnel of favor and fear and now they were his. That was the blessing and the curse: he could count on them because he could crush them.

On the TV in the corner, muted, Tracy Rockefeller smiled for a crowd in the plaza in front of Rockefeller Center. Confederations of balloons trembled behind her. Her running mate stood at a cautious distance, already calculating a future of his own.

Someone said, tentative, "Sir, we should game out Jan—"

"January sixth?" Hawley's smile showed teeth. "That was amateur hour," he said. "We won't fuck it up this time."

The silence came with a hard edge. Even the clock hesitated.

"For the good of the country," Hawley said, and the men around him nodded because that was the phrase that made questionable things sound noble.

"Tell everyone we are headed to Camp David," Hawley barked before heading out across the lawn to Marine One.

As Hawley boarded Marine One, he handed the pilot a piece of paper with "Raven Rock" written on it. The pilot nodded, the door closed, the rotors spun up, and the White House became a receding dot in the night.

Early Evening - Rockefeller Center – New York City

Tracy Rockefeller stood in the family's private suite, a room that pretended not to be grand. The carpets were soft enough to swallow footsteps. Floor-to-ceiling windows looked onto an ocean of lights and flags. Somewhere below, an ice rink gleamed like a postage stamp.

"Madam President-elect," said her chief of staff, breathless with caution, "we need to consider—"

"I'm not president-elect until every vote is counted," Tracy said, and because she believed in the sentence, it did not sound like a line.

On the coffee table, three phones vibrated in a jittery waltz. Her daughter Elle picked one up, frowned, picked up another. A lock of hair fell over her cheek; she pushed it away with the back of her wrist, eyes narrowed.

"Mom," Elle said quietly. "Come here."

As Tracy was walking over to Elle, she said into her phone, "Thanks George, but I hope this is all unnecessary" before hanging up.

They moved to a corner near a painting—something abstract in whites and grays. Elle angled her phone. A map winked to life. A pulsing blue dot glowed amid contour lines and green splotches.

"Jimmy," Elle said. "He never turned off location sharing."

Tracy's mouth tightened. "I thought you blocked him."

"I did," Elle said. "But he shows up under 'Family.' He never removed me."

Tracy couldn't help it; she laughed once, a dry huff. "Men."

Elle zoomed the map with two fingers. Above the dot, a label flickered: Blue Ridge Summit, Pennsylvania. She tapped, pulled up a name even people who followed politics didn't know. "Raven Rock," she said. "Site R."

Tracy looked at the blue dot again. It beat like a heart.

"Where's the President?" Elle asked.

The chief of staff was already at the glass doors, talking to Secret Service. Faces hardened. An agent with a face like a carefully closed book came in close. "Ma'am, with your permission, we're moving you to a secure location."

Tracy glanced back at the TV. On the screen, the bottom-of-the-hour chatter had quieted, a text block teasing Special Address. "Now?" she said.

"Now," the agent said.

News cut through the sky like a lightning strike.

On one network a panel stopped mid-sentence as an amber banner rolled: BREAKING: PRESIDENT TO ADDRESS NATION. On another, footage from a protest in Milwaukee cut off as the feed switched to the seal, the music, the breathless pivot. Phones across the country chirped with push notifications. The words "The President will announce he has ordered the vote count suspended" trended and then spiked.

On the street outside Rockefeller Center, horns answered each other like animals. Down in Atlanta, a line of protestors met a line of riot police beneath the gold dome. In Phoenix, a woman with a bullhorn invoked her grandfather who had fled a different kind of emergency decree. In Boise, men loaded long guns into truck beds under a sky with too many stars.

A major general whose name would be forgotten appeared only as a silhouette on a network that promised to protect him. "We do not obey illegal orders," he said, voice filtered, and the anchor blinked hard and thanked him and the feed cut back to the smiling headshot they used for Hawley.

In living rooms in Queens and kitchens in Tulsa and on back porches in El Paso, people asked the same question with different words: What now?

Early Evening – Raven Rock - November 3, 2036

The flag in the corner didn't move. It couldn't; the air in the bunker was filtered and still. President Ted Hawley rested his fingertips on the Resolute Desk and stared into the lens as if he could reach through it into every living room in America.

"My fellow Americans," he said, voice wrapped in sympathy, "we are under attack."

On the prompter, the words crawled calm and relentless. *Under attack, safeguard democracy, suspend the vote count, foreign interference.* The camera light was a green pupil reflected in his eyes. Off to the side, an oil portrait of George Washington watched with borrowed authority. The lighting was perfect, the drapery exact, the rug a flawless replica— thirteen stars in a neat circle.

"Effective immediately," Hawley continued, "I have taken necessary steps to safeguard our democracy. We cannot allow subversion to steal the voice of the people. Therefore, I have ordered the vote count suspended until we can root out all fraud and ballot box tampering."

The cameraman's hand rose: three, two, one—cut.

Hawley let the smile die on his face. He looked upward, not at a ceiling fresco but at poured concrete and steel. The hum that threaded through the room came from air handlers, not late-night White House plumbing. He'd had the replica built to an obsessive standard, right down to the scratches on the desk. But there was no sun outside this Oval Office and never would be.

An aide stepped forward with a tablet. "Mr. President, the major networks are carrying it. The socials will follow."

"They'll follow the volume," Hawley said. "Make sure we're the loudest."

Another aide approached, younger, pale. "Sir, the first action—uh—encountered… resistance."

"Which action?"

"Rockefeller," the aide said, throat working. "We... didn't get her."

Hawley's jaw ticked. He smoothed the lapel of his dark suit, re-centering the flag pin.

"Find her," he said softly, and the softness made the aide flinch. "Find her and bring her to me. Alive. Do you understand?"

"Yes, sir."

Hawley turned back to the camera—the eye he preferred. "Run it again," he said. "This time clip the opening for socials. Thirty seconds. Make me sound like Washington."

Early Evening – The Townhouse - Washington D.C.

The townhouse sat between a consulate and a boutique that pretended to be a bookshop. Brick and ivy. A brass knocker in the shape of a lion's head. Inside, the air held the smell of wax and old paper and money that had been in rooms like this for two centuries.

Harry Bell's phone buzzed once. He didn't keep it on the table; he was not the sort of man who needed to see his name light up glass. He excused himself, stepped into the paneled hall, and answered.

"Bell," he said.

"Washington is going to need your help," said the voice on the line.

No preamble. No honorifics. The phrase was a stone dropped in still water.

"I agree," Bell said simply, and returned to the table.

Twelve faces lifted, some familiar to a passing world, most carefully obscure. They did not use their names here. They used their states. Rhode Island's hands were steepled. Georgia's eyes were wet. New York's cufflinks were small silver arrows.

"Ladies and gentlemen," Bell said, "the Chief Justice is on his way."

At the far end of the table sat an empty chair, the Chief Justice's Chair, with a coaster resting on its arm. It had been empty for years at a time. That was the point. This group existed best when it did not need to exist at all.

Election Day Evening - The Townhouse

The knock was a small thing. The reaction was not. The dozen people around the table sat straighter. Bell rose from the head of the table and moved to the door himself. He never delegated the important rituals.

Chief Justice Anthony Hoyt looked tired in the way that comes from carrying something heavy you can't set down. He shook Bell's hand and stepped inside. He was dressed like a man down on his luck and likely in need of a warm meal. That was the point, no one gave him a second look on the street. However, Hoyt had made sure to be seen at the Court earlier in the evening, strolling down the marble steps for the benefit of three cameras. A decoy's shadow.

He reached into the inner pocket of his coat and took out an envelope the color of tea. Three red wax seals glinted like old blood. The faces around the table didn't breathe.

"Colleagues," Hoyt said, using the only term that felt equal enough, "it is my duty to inform you that the conditions described by President Washington and Chief Justice John Jay in the instrument known to you as the Washington Amendment—the Decree —have been met."

He set the envelope on the table and removed his hand. The wax caught a light and shone.

"By the instrument, only the Chief Justice may invoke it," he said. "By tradition, I ask whether you accept invocation."

The room was so quiet they could hear an ambulance siren miles away, cutting through the city like a needle.

Going by the same order in which each state had signed the original Declaration of Independence, New Hampshire's voice threaded with steel. "We accept."

One by one the others answered each in their cadence. "We accept." "We accept." A chorus, a vow. Bell waited for the twelfth and then he made it thirteen.

"We have not intervened at all since 1974," Hoyt said softly, "and even then, it was quietly behind the scenes. Never before have we been asked to fully invoke Washington's Decree."

"Then," Hoyt continued, "let me tell you where the powers behind the decree live."

He gave them a name and a mechanism—a box within a box within a bell. He gave them a code that wasn't numbers or letters but a pattern of stars.

"And if we don't retrieve it?" Georgia asked.

"Then we are a story that will never be told," Hoyt said. "Stories do not command armies. With the Decree and Washington's enduring military preeminence and seniority—we have the power of the law on our side. Without the decree and the powers it gives, it's only a long forgotten tale."

Election Day Evening - Rockefeller Center

"Move," said the agent with the closed-book face.

Tracy's chief of staff had already palmed a small key and opened a panel that looked like part of the wall. Behind it, an old elevator winked awake. The agents formed a box around Tracy and Elle, hustling them across the room as the televised seal gave way to Hawley's face.

"My fellow Americans…"

Tracy caught a last glimpse of the screen as the elevator doors swallowed them. Hawley's mouth formed vote and suspended, and somewhere below, the gears engaged and the car slid down.

Elle's hand found hers in the dark. "He's underground," Elle whispered. "That's why Jimmy's in Pennsylvania."

Tracy squeezed back. Her voice, when it came, was steady. "If Hawley has gone underground, then we need to too, he's likely sending people to grab us. If he's making a grab for power, he's going to want us under his control."

They descended past floors that weren't in any fire code diagram, into a garage that smelled like hot rubber and old secrets. An agent opened the rear door of a black sedan. Tracy ducked in, Elle behind her, the door shutting with a soft, expensive click.

As the sedan crept along a service corridor, a different set of black SUVs rolled up to the front of 30 Rock, lights off. Men with earpieces moved quickly across the lobby and into the elevators.

They were 5 minutes late.

By the time they reached the private suite, the room was empty but for the soft chiming of abandoned phones. An aide's coffee cooled beside a half-eaten almond. On the television, Hawley promised safety.

"Where are they?" the lead agent snapped.

"Gone," a janitor said, voice shaking. "She has a private entrance—"

"Where?" The lead agent demanded.

"I don't know, they just disappeared", the janitor stated.

The lead agent's jaw flexed. "Seal the exits. Scrub the feeds."

He didn't say find them because that was the only verb anyone was using tonight.

Election Day Evening - The Townhouse

The thirteen did not hold hands. They were not that kind of group. But the air between them tightened like a rope.

Bell slid the sealed ancient envelope back toward Hoyt. The Chief Justice broke the first seal and then stopped. He did not open the document itself. He knew it by heart. That was the point of the ritual: the words lived in a human head as well as a lockbox.

"The terms are simple," Hoyt said. "We act to preserve the Constitution, not to supplant it. We remove threats and we return power."

"And the targets?" asked New York.

Hoyt looked at Bell. It would be Bell's job to say the names aloud.

"Hawley is attempting to nullify a lawful election by stopping the vote count," Bell said. "It will only be a matter of time before he calls out the National Guard". "We need to be prepared in case he attempts to declare martial law."

"Who is currently supporting him?" asked Pennsylvania—the general with the straight back and the unflinching eyes.

"The Chairman of the Joint Chiefs, the VP, the Speaker of the House, the Attorney General" Hoyt said.

"And the other Supreme Court Justices?" Rhode Island asked.

Hoyt didn't answer. He didn't need to, they all knew 2 members of Hoyt's court would come down on Hawley's side.

Bell tapped the envelope with one fingertip. "We retrieve the decree," he said. "We need to find Rockefeller. We countermand illegal orders with legal ones and, if needed, we will use force. We do not break the American experiment to save it."

Across the table, Massachusetts—the Associate Justice—exhaled. "And if we fail?"

Bell's smile didn't reach his eyes. "Then there are no more meetings."

Election Day Evening - Raven Rock

Hawley watched the attempts come back to him as bullet points. TARGET LOC. MISSED. ROUTE UNKNOWN.CONTACTS COMPROMISED. SOCIAL SENTIMENT: VOLATILE.

He closed his eyes and pictured the map. He had been raised on maps—oil leases and river rights and counties that could be bought with a handshake if the hand was the right hand. He had learned that lines were only as real as the men who enforced them.

"Sir," Bragg said, measured, respectful. "I would advise caution."

"I didn't ask for advice," Hawley said, and opened his eyes. "I asked for results."

Bragg's gaze flickered to Clark, to McCollins, to Harris, a silent communion of men who had discovered they were smaller than the machine they had helped build. Bragg then stated quietly, "Under Title 32, the Guard answers to governors unless federalized under the Insurrection Act. Posse Comitatus still binds the regulars. We need a predicate."

"Be ready to do it if we need to. In the meanwhile, find me Tracy Rockefeller." Hawley snorted back.

He looked back at the portrait of Washington, a copy hung to make speeches weightier.

"You ought to appreciate this," Hawley told the first president softly. "Order. Discipline. Continuity."

The hum of the bunker answered him. Somewhere in the concrete heart of the mountain, a door shut.

Election Day Evening – Rockefeller Center

As the motorcade slipped out of a forgotten back loading dock two blocks from Rockefeller Center, Tracy watched the city flicker past in slices—loading docks, stacked crates, a cat startled into flight. She felt for Elle's hand again, found it, held on.

"We'll go to ground," the agent said from the front seat. "We have sites."

"We have friends," Tracy said. "More important."

Elle looked at her phone, at the pulsing dot in the Pennsylvania hills. "Jimmy's not moving," she murmured. "He's in place."

Tracy nodded once. It was all she needed to know.

Above them, on screens in a million windows, the President spoke about order while the country was waiting for a final count that he was determined to prevent.

Election Day Late Evening - The Townhouse

Bell looked around the table and saw not power but responsibility mapped onto faces. Their diversity was not a photograph's caption but a set of tools he could use. Each represented a different lever that he could pull hard.

"Virginia," he said, and a governor sat forward. "Find out if we can secure safe transit corridors west, across the Virginias. Quietly." Washington owned land in the Ohio River Valley that he left to us and if we need to move, we have safe haven there.

"Pennsylvania," to the general. "In time we will need loyal units and eyes on Raven Rock." Who can we count on?

"New York," to the lawyer. "Draft the injunctions that should not be needed but will be. Draft the orders Hoyt will then sign to slow Hawley down."

"Georgia. Rhode Island. Maryland. South Carolina…" He gave each an assignment— media choke points, financial valves, communications nets, develop our plans for each.

Bell ended with himself. "Hoyt and I will retrieve Washington's Decree."

Hoyt put a hand on the envelope, then on Bell's shoulder, a weight and a benediction. "Let's go," he said.

They rose and headed off to their assigned tasks.

Election Day Late Evening - Raven Rock

"Sir," the aide said, voice thin. "The first attempt failed."

Hawley's rage was a quiet thing. The truly dangerous emotions always were. He rolled his shoulders once; the motion of a fighter who has decided a bout has gone long enough.

"Then we keep going," he said. "Find the girl. Find the mother. Find whoever thinks they can tell me no."

He looked at the camera he'd just addressed, its glass blank and watchful.

"Line up the next speech," he said. "Make it shorter. Make it harder. We need to start exerting power."

Outside, beyond rock and wire and layers of men with guns, November settled on the capital like a held breath.

In a city of townhouses, one room went dark. In a mountain, one replica Oval Office glowed brighter. Between them, a country teetered, and thirteen people stepped forward to hold a line no one else could see.

Election Day Late Evening - The Townhouse

"…when the voice of faction drowns the voice of the People, prudence requires a sentinel beyond faction."— from a private note in George Washington's hand, 1794

The townhouse's boardroom felt older in the morning light. The moonlight dragged across the table like a slow searchlight, catching dust in solemn orbits. The envelope with the three wax seals sat between Chief Justice Hoyt and Harry Bell as if it had always been there, as if the furniture had been built around it.

"Before we move," Hoyt said, "you asked for the whole of it. Origins. Rules. History. You deserve to know what you are invoking."

No one picked up a pen. They listened the way juries listen when the outcome touches bone.

"Washington's fear wasn't paranoia," Hoyt went on. "He watched revolutions curdle. He watched men who loved power more than the law. In 1794, a year into his second term, he asked John Jay for a guarantee—quiet and small—a decree that would carry with it permanent authority."

Bell nodded once. He had seen a photocopy of the letter only twice in his life, then watched it burn.

"They called it—in Washington and Jay's own hand—*the Decree*," Hoyt said. They sometimes, mistakenly, called it the Washington Amendment, but it could never be an official amendment as it could not be public. Instead, they crafted a decree with the power of an amendment, entrusted to the Chief Justice and to thirteen Americans drawn from the original states. Jay drafted it and personally gathered signatures from the thirteen state governors, the President Pro Tempore of the Senate, the Speaker of the House, the Chief Justice, and finally President Washington. With that last seal, the Thirteen Guarantors existed."

He touched the envelope with two fingers, not opening it. "Washington was practical. The first Guarantors, in 1794, were the senior senators from each original state—men already trusted by their states, chosen for merit, commitment to republican government, and service to independence."

Hoyt's voice slowed, became the cadence of something memorized long ago. "The rules were simple."

"First: The Guarantors are sworn to the Constitution alone, and to restore it when usurped."

"Second: The Guarantors act only when the Constitution is threatened, including if a President refuses to yield lawful succession or dissolves the People's representation."

"Third: Appointment is for life; succession is by sealed designation, held by the *first among equals*."

"Fourth: Only the Chief Justice holds the key and knows the decree; he alone may invoke the Decree and charge the Guarantors to take action."

"Fifth: Remove the threat, then return power to its lawful channels at the earliest hour."

"Sixth: Treason by a Guarantor is put to a vote of ten; mercy is not mandated or expected."

"Seventh: They meet officially only once every four years, upon a peaceful oath, to toast the Experiment. In all other times, they do not exist."

Rhode Island—Teruel—said softly, "and that's the way we have always wanted it kept."

"We have," Hoyt said. "And we have been sparing. In two and a half centuries, there have been only a few quiet interventions."

He raised a hand and, as if cueing a projector, gave them brief, bright vignettes.

"Post–Franklin Roosevelt's tenure: We concluded custom wouldn't hold. We pressed—quietly—for presidential term limits. The Twenty-Second Amendment walked the path we cleared."

"January 1974: Watergate. By unanimous judgment, a President who had tried to bend the law had to go. The courts sufficed, and Nixon was forced from power."

"We also convened outside our formal four year cadence but without national activation," he added. "April 1861—two members defected to the Confederacy; we purged them internally. And January 2021, after the Capitol was attacked. The checks held; we did not act."

The air around the table felt heavy. The present pressed in.

"And before all those," Bell said quietly, "there were the original Thirteen."

Hoyt nodded. "The roster Washington and Jay compiled in 1794 listed the senior senators who would carry the coin for each state: Massachusetts — Caleb Strong. Connecticut — Oliver Ellsworth. New York — Aaron Burr. New Hampshire — John Langdon. Rhode Island — Joseph Stanton. New Jersey — John Rutherfurd. Pennsylvania — Robert Morris. Delaware — George

Read. Maryland — John Henry. Virginia — James Monroe. North Carolina — Samuel Johnston. South Carolina — Pierce Butler. Georgia — James Gunn."

"Men who had already sworn twice," Pennsylvania said—the general's voice steady. "First to independence. Then to the Constitution."

"And they then swore a third time," Hoyt said. "In a parlor at Mount Vernon, with Washington's seal in wax and Jay's ink still damp."

He looked down the table at the modern faces. "The roster has evolved by design—governors, senators, military leaders, business and finance—so the tools fit the times. But the promise is unchanged."

Bell went around the table, not with titles but with the economy of a deployment.

"Virginia," he said to Governor Bill McLean. "Delaware—Governor Kathy Curtis. Rhode Island—John Teruel. Connecticut—Harry Bell Pennsylvania—General Charles Taylor. Massachusetts—Justice Walter Lockwood. New Hampshire—Senator Susan Lewis. Georgia—Lynn Tyler. New York—Nate Burr. New Jersey—Julia Jackson. Maryland—Sam Fitzwilliams. North Carolina—George Damon. South Carolina—Professor Jennifer Remington."

Thirteen faces. Thirteen levers. The modern roster breathed as one organism.

Hoyt added, "One more piece of the machinery. Washington intended that our invoking of his standing military authority be the core of our power in a crisis. In 1776, Congress appointed him *'General and Commander in Chief of the army of the United States and of all the forces raised or to be raised by them.'* And in 1976, Congress named him General of the Armies—posthumously and permanently—ensuring he remains the senior military officer of the

United States. When the Decree is lawfully invoked by the Chief Justice, Washington's precedence anchors obedience in the chain of command."

Bell let out a breath he hadn't known he'd kept. "Washington's hand remains ever present on the levers of power."

Hoyt nodded once. "Exactly."

"We need to go," Bell said. "Retrieve the box."

New York—Burr—raised a hand. "One thing before you go. *Why Lawrence Washington's tomb?* Of all places."

Hoyt met his eye. "Because George Washington needed a hiding place that would last, would be guarded, and would likely go undisturbed for centuries. His half brother Lawrence's vault checked all three—on family ground, tended by caretakers, protected by reverence, and too humble to invite rifling."

Burr's mouth tilted. "The new tomb is a shrine. The old one is a secret."

"Exactly," Hoyt said. "What better place to bury a secret than a tomb."

Very Late Night – Mount Vernon

Mount Vernon did not look like a place where a modern republic would come to be saved. It had the composed beauty of postcards: white colonnade, red roof, the Potomac shouldering past in flat gray sheets. But the stillness was a trick. History had laid traps here. The estate slept with one eye open.

They went at night. Optics mattered. Hoyt traded his tie for a dark scarf and a worn peacoat that made him look like a professor again. Bell dressed the way billionaires dress when they want to disappear; navy cap, salt-gray coat, shoes that cost more than most cars and didn't look it. A single SUV, windows as dark as they could make them.

They had a map, but not the gift shop kind. Hoyt had sketched the paths from memory: the slope down past the smokehouse, the slight U in the gravel where heavy caskets once passed, the line of hollies like sentries.

"The old vault," Hoyt murmured as they walked. "Washington wrote to his nephew about it. Called it 'unworthy' of the General. The new tomb was built later. But Lawrence—he is in the old one still."

"Lawrence," Bell repeated, letting the name steady him.

They reached the Old Tomb as fog lifted in a soft shroud from the river. It was humble: a low brick vault set into the earth, barred by an iron grate with a lock that belonged in a museum.

"Security?" Bell asked.

"Rotates," Hoyt said. "And they're not expecting pilgrims who know which shadow to stand in." He checked his watch. "Four minutes after the hour, the guard pauses at the mansion to log. It's been true for thirty years. Tradition is the most reliable predictor."

Bell produced a key that wasn't a key—flat, matte, with teeth like a comet's tail.

The old lock surrendered with a sigh, as if relieved to be part of the story again.

Inside, lantern light licked across the uneven brick. Two sarcophagus-like forms rested beyond, simple and spare. The air had that cool, mineral quality of places that keep their own time.

Hoyt didn't step forward first. He bowed his head in a gesture that didn't read as piety so much as respect. "We are here, General," he said—not to George, but to the first Washington to lie here. "We are here for what your brother protected."

Bell crouched at the threshold. He had always liked puzzles more than he liked people. On the iron grate itself, a detail most tourists never saw: twelve iron rosettes, each hammered into a petal-pointed star. Not thirteen. Twelve.

"Washington's rose," Bell said. "The compass points."

Hoyt smiled the kind of smile that didn't use his mouth. "A rose with a missing petal so the eye searches for what is not there."

He pointed to the lintel: chiseled into the brick, worn to a whisper, the faint circle of thirteen stars. Not arranged in the familiar simple ring, but in a pattern that looked random until it didn't.

"Box within a box within a bell," Hoyt said, recalling the clue he'd offered in the townhouse. "We press the stars in the order of the old flag code. The thirteenth is the bell."

Bell reached up and pressed the first star in the pattern where the faintest of scrapes marked a century of someone else's touch. It depressed with a click. He found the second, the third. Metal whispered. When he pressed the twelfth, somewhere inside the brick a latch rearranged its mind.

"Where's the thirteenth?" Bell asked.

Hoyt tilted his lantern. In the upper corner, nearly lost to soot, a star had not been carved but *painted* long ago—an empty absence now. "The thirteenth isn't a star," he said softly. "It's a sound."

He tugged a small hemp rope hidden in the corner, and a gentle tone answered from within the vault, one note as pure as winter.

Bell blinked. "You put a bell in a tomb."

"Jay did," Hoyt said. "He had a sense of humor."

A brick near the floor gave up its weight. Bell eased it free. Behind, a narrow cavity. Within the cavity, an object wrapped in oilcloth and tied with a ribbon turned the color of old tea.

Bell slid it out. The package was smaller than he'd imagined—shoebox length, not Bible-thick—but heavy with density that wasn't only material. He unwrapped it on his knees, careful, reverent in a way he would not have recognized in himself twenty years ago.

The inner box was made of beech softened by two and a half centuries of secrets. On its lid, a wax seal intact despite time: a circle of thirteen stars and the faint impression of Washington's crest. Beneath that, another seal—a jurist's scales. Jay's.

Hoyt laid a hand on the lid and closed his eyes. "Hello, old friend."

He broke the seals with a thumbnail and lifted.

Inside: a vellum folded into thirds, edges darkened not by fire but by oil from hands that had done heavy work. A small leather wallet holding a ring of keys that were not keys—coin-thin, each stamped with a state and a year. A packet of four letters bound with twine, each sealed in red wax and addressed in a steady 18th-century hand: *To the Commanding Officer — United States Army*; *To the Commanding Officer — United States Navy*; *To the Speaker of the House*; *To the President of the Senate*. Tucked into a corner, a loop of cord from which hung a pewter charm in the shape of a bell. The clapper was a sliver of silver. When Bell touched it, it sang, almost inaudible.

Hoyt unfolded the vellum. The script marched neat and slow across the page.

To the Chief Justice of the United States and to the Thirteen Guarantors of the Constitution.

He didn't read it aloud. He had read it aloud once before—in a basement in a different crisis. He scanned until he found the clause that mattered most.

"To be invoked when the Constitution is threatened, a President refuses to yield lawful power or abrogates the People's representation. In such times… you are empowered to take all necessary action to restore in haste the lawful government as defined by the constitution."

Bell breathed out. "No poetry."

"Washington didn't need poetry," Hoyt said. "He needed to give direction. And a bridge to lawful force."

Bell lifted the four sealed letters, weighing each. "Contingencies," he said. "Direct lines to the sword, the fleet, and the two keystones of Congress."

"And to offices, not men," Hoyt added. "Whichever hands hold them in that hour. Each letter cites Washington's standing precedence—his 1776 appointment as Commander in Chief and his 1976 elevation as General of the Armies—explicitly so that when I lawfully invoke the Decree, obedience can flow down the chain of command."

Bell turned one envelope in his hands, feeling the grit of old wax. "Authority that spans time."

Hoyt nodded. "Washington's commission never expired. In 1976 Congress made it explicit—General of the Armies. When I invoke the Decree, his rank speaks through the law, and the law still speaks to soldiers."

From outside the vault came the distant burr of tires on gravel. They froze. Hoyt extinguished the lantern. Darkness moved in.

A flashlight cone skimmed the trees beyond the path. A security guard made his rounds, his footsteps steady, bored. He paused at the mansion to sign a clipboard with a pen attached by a chain. Tradition is the most reliable calendar.

The light slid away. The night exhaled.

"Let's not test our luck," Hoyt whispered.

They re-wrapped the beech box, slid the loose brick back into place, and reset the iron rosette stars, the latch whispering its agreement. Hoyt tugged the hidden rope. The little bell made its single clear note. The vault resumed its expression of mute patience.

They locked the grate and melted into the shadows.

By the time the guard ambled past the old vault, the air smelled only of cold and river.

Very Late Night – SUV

Back in the SUV, Bell rested the box on his knees as if it were a fragile child. The road out of Mount Vernon twisted under trees that had learned to keep secrets.

"Funding," Hoyt said suddenly, as if remembering a stray but crucial cog. "The brief mentioned a river of money."

Bell nodded, eyes on the dark ribbon of road. "Washington seeded a fund in plain sight. Later, it moved through the Manhattan Company—Aaron Burr's trick with water charters and banks. Over centuries, names changed, mergers swallowed mergers. The Manhattan Water Company became The Bank of Manhattan, but the account never closed. The interest it generates today alone could move mountains, if one knew it existed and how to access it."

"And the access today?"

"You," Hoyt said without malice.

Bell huffed once, a laugh ground down to grit. "I've always known the account existed, and when we get back to the townhouse, so will all the others."

Hoyt glanced at him. "You see why you were chosen."

The SUV crested a rise. Beyond, the low clouds over Washington glowed bruise-blue with city light. Somewhere under that dome of reflection, protests still threaded streets, speeches still curled through microphones, and orders—legal and not—still flew like migrating birds.

Bell touched the pewter charm again. It sang back the faintest of replies.

Very Late Night – The Townhouse

The townhouse was like a medieval cathedral. Dark, silent, and full of secrets.

They unwrapped the box and placed it in the center of the table. The Thirteen leaned in, not crowding so much as converging. The air tightened.

"Read it please," New Jersey said.

Bell did not read the whole; he read the parts that made the instrument a machine: the invocation clause; the authority to countermand illegal orders; the instruction to communicate to governors, to marshals, to commanders the lawfulness of refusal. He read the line that had cost men sleep in every century since it was written:

"To fail to act when action is required is to betray the People whom we serve."

Bell set the four sealed letters beside the vellum, so the addressees were visible. Even the seasoned among them went still.

"Those go only if we must," Bell said. "Army. Navy. Speaker. President of the Senate. They are to be delivered under the Chief Justice's seal and the Guarantors' concurrence.

New York reached for the coin-key stamped with his state. Massachusetts palmed his. Pennsylvania—Taylor—took his and weighed it as if testing the heft of a promise. One by one, the Thirteen collected the coins that were older than their grandparents' grandparents, and suddenly the centuries did not feel like legend. They felt like continuity and understood the gravity

"Chief," Bell said—the title that mattered tonight. "You'll sign the first orders when we are ready?"

Burr – New York, nodded. "I have already drafted two for the Chief to sign. One is a directive to federal judges to fast-track all habeas petitions for unlawful detentions and to enjoin any executive actions that impede certification. The second is a memorandum to the governors clarifying the limits of federal authority under the Insurrection Act without legislated triggers." He tapped the vellum's margin. "And this gives them the backbone."

Julia Jackson—New Jersey—looked from the vellum to the faces around the table, a broadcaster assessing an audience before a hard segment. "You know Hawley will ignore the court's orders and try to have you arrested."

"I know," Hoyt said. "And I will be prepared."

"We need to make Hawley show his hand," Bell said. "The quicker the better, remember we are watching him, but he has no idea we exist."

As the Guarantors began to head to their private quarters, buried securely beneath the townhouse—Bell caught Hoyt's sleeve. "One more thing," he said. "There were thirteen stars on the lintel, but only twelve rosettes. Why make the thirteenth a bell?"

Hoyt's eyes found the pewter charm. He smiled, small and tired and a little proud of men who had been dead two hundred and fifty years. "Because there are moments a nation needs to be rung awake," he said.

The door closed on them one by one, and the townhouse held its breath.

Outside, sirens braided with chants. The city trembled on its axis. In a mountain, a man rehearsed a shorter, harder speech. In a centuries old vault by the river, a tiny bell vibrated itself back to stillness.

Day 2 - The Big Unfolding

Just After Midnight - Manhattan

The motorcade hit Eleventh Avenue like a black river—three SUVs tight, two sedans wide, lights low, horns silent. Sirens wailed somewhere else, for someone else. New York's night reflected back at them in a thousand panes of glass.

"West Side," the lead agent said into his sleeve. "Then north."

Tracy Rockefeller sat behind tinted glass and watched her own reflection cut by streetlights. Beside her, Elle's hands were quiet on her lap, thumbs still over the screen that had shown them what mattered: Jimmy's blue dot pulsing in Pennsylvania. Across from them, two agents they trusted—Vega and Whitman—tracked the world beyond the glass with predator calm.

At Thirty-Second Street the convoy slid right, northbound lanes yawning open. At Twenty-Fourth, without a word, the middle SUV blinked once and drifted left. Twenty-Third they slipped out from under the umbrella of their own security.

"Hold steady," Vega said, easing the wheel. The decoy stream rolled on without them, three dark boxes gaining speed, the lead car's rear glass catching a slice of Tracy's face one last time, then losing it to distance.

They crossed Eleventh and turned south.

"Phones," Tracy said, suddenly, flat and calm. "All of them. Now."

Whitman's head snapped, then he was already digging. Elle handed hers over without looking at it; Tracy took it and her own in one hand and with the other pulled a soft graphite-gray pouch from her bag—sleek, zippered, unbranded.

"Faraday," she said, more to the habit than to the men, and dropped hers and Elle's into the bag, zipped, folded the flap, pressed the strip shut.

Vega passed his up. Whitman hesitated a fraction—old muscle memory—then surrendered his. Tracy weighed both, then pressed them into Elle's palm.

"Two trucks," she said. "Backs open. Different directions."

As if the city heard her, two delivery trucks rumbled past in parallel—the first with its roll-up door braced half-open as it idled for a loading dock, the second with a rear canvas curtain clipped back. Vega cracked the rear window. Elle leaned, judged the gap, and let Vega pace them. One flick—clean arc into cardboard and pallets. Two breaths later, she slid the second into the curtain's pocket of shadow. Both trucks kept going north, faithful little ghosts.

Whitman rolled the window up and exhaled through his nose. "That'll create a bit of noise and distraction."

"It'll buy us time," Tracy said. "Any noise is a bonus."

The city changed flavors block by block—the galleries asleep behind iron gates, the meatpackers' last forklifts clanking to a stop, the river beginning to smell like iron and salt. At Pier 59 the security booth was empty, the marina office dark. Vega pulled up to a roll-up door flaking with aging graffiti. It groaned just enough to make them flinch, then rose.

The unmarked garage smelled like rubber and dust. Vega backed the SUV into a shadow between two columns. Whitman tugged a tarp over it, then pulled a corrugated panel down on a set of tracks, making the bay look like a closet that had always been closed.

"Move," he said softly.

They went out on foot, heads down against a cutter of wind that came off the water like news. The pier planks knocked quietly under their boots. Past a row of masts, past a boat with a party's balloons surrendering one by one to the night, past a small sign that said CHELSEA PIERS MARINA in letters that pretended this was all simple.

Slip C-12 held a Beneteau Oceanis Yacht with a hull the color of bleached pine. The name on the transom was modest: Mistral.

Vega sprang aboard first, then reached for Elle. Tracy followed, moving like a woman still deciding to trust her sea legs. Whitman unlooped the shore power with careful hands, coiled it as if he'd been doing this his whole life.

Tracy knew enough to stay out of Vega's way as he checked the fuel, the bilge, the seacocks. She ducked into the cockpit, found the ignition, and listened for the tiny pause that told her the glow plugs had warmed. The Yanmar turned over and came alive, a low, contented rumble.

"Lines," she said.

Elle was already at the cleats. Spring line first, then stern. She left the bow for last, fingers quick, a little white at the knuckles. Whitman cast off the final loop and stepped aboard in one liquid motion. Vega eased the throttle, thumb on the bow thruster. The hull shouldered free of the dock with a push that felt like relief.

They ghosted past the empty slips with only running lights and the marina's tired gulls to watch them. The current took them gently by the shoulder and pointed them south. Off their port beam, the High Line's bones glowed faintly, a thin ribcage over old rail.

"Stay with the ebb," Vega murmured, not because Tracy needed the advice—she understood the Hudson's moods—but because saying it made them participants in something other than escape. They were sailors. Sailors talked about tide.

"VHF to sixteen," Whitman said. "AIS… leave it on. We need to look like what we want them to believe."

"Just another boat headed south for the winter," Elle said, and the sentence warmed the space around them.

Chelsea's lights fell behind. The river widened into the city's open mouth. There were other movements in the dark—a dinner cruise churning bubbles under a glass roof, a tug snorting at a barge like a bull at a gate.

They slid past the ghost of the Titanic's intended pier. The skyline leaned inward, curious. At the Battery, the wind checked them and Tracy feathered the throttle. Ahead, the Verrazzano's twin towers stood up out of the water like a doorway, lit and inevitable.

"Security call, outbound container at Bergen Point," a voice crackled on sixteen, bored and professional. The normalcy of it made Elle breathe. "Security, inbound ferry Whitehall, two minutes to slip."

They tucked themselves on the hip of a tug, hiding a little in its bigger purpose. The wake slapped Mistral's hull with flat hands. On Governor's Island, a single light turned on in a window and then off again, someone deciding to go back to bed.

Vega kept his eyes on the chart plotter and his ears on the water. "Ambrose," he said to Tracy. "Take the channel, then bail to the Jersey side. No need to tempt a helicopter."

"Copy," she said, and the word felt like home.

Very Early Morning - Taconic Parkway - NY State

Behind them, in a different version of the night, three black SUVs ran north with too much confidence. The lead driver kept his foot pinned to the accelerator. They took the Henry Hudson to the Saw Mill, then cut to the Taconic as if by sheer will they could beat whatever might be coming for them.

They never made it to Pocantico Hills.

A road flare threw violent orange at the trees. A work crew's arrow board blinked LEFT LEFT LEFT. The motorcade shot past and a second later the world constricted: unmarked cruisers at the shoulder, a box truck angled just wrong, men in plain black stepping out with blank faces and clipped earpieces.

The lead agent braked hard, tires howling. Doors banged open. Hawley's men moved with the choreographed certainty of people who had rehearsed this in a warehouse in Virginia.

"On the ground!" someone shouted. It didn't matter who.

Hands showed. Knees found gravel. A flashlight found the interior of the middle SUV and flooded leather that was empty of the two faces that mattered. Hawley's lead—a strong man with a weak future—swore into his microphone.

"Decoy," he said. "They're not here."

"Where?" The voice that came back was very calm.

He swallowed. "We don't know."

The calm voice did not answer. Somewhere else, underground, a hand that believed it controlled the world marked a new target on a map.

Very Early Morning - Mistral

On the Hudson, the night said nothing. Mistral knifed under the Verrazzano as if passing through a ring. The sea opened up, a black plane cut by white scribbles of foam. They could have turned left for the Narrows or right for the Kill van Kull, but Vega held them straight. South. Away.

Elle stood in the companionway with a hand on the lintel and watched the Statue of Liberty's lamp carve a little hole in the dark. "She looks smaller from the water," she said.

"Everything looks smaller from the water," Whitman said.

"Where are we going?" Elle asked softly.

"Chesapeake," Tracy said. "Or farther. Boats run south this time of year. If we're another one, we're no one."

Vega, watching the ghost shapes of buoys, said, "We'll make the hook at Sandy and decide. There's a man at Cape May who owes me a meal."

"Does he know he owes you a life?" Elle asked.

"Not yet," Vega said, and smiled without any joy.

They kept to the edge of the lane to make themselves easy to explain and hard to touch. Once, a spotlight combed the water from a patrol boat near Fort Wadsworth and found them and swept past, uninterested. Once, a chopper thudded across the black with a sound that made hearts hunch, but it was dragging its tail inland, toward a city that would not sleep.

Whitman brought up a thermos and paper cups. Coffee steam curled into air so cold it hurt. Elle wrapped both hands around hers and let the heat choose her.

"I always thought it would be a train," she said to no one. "If we had to run. Something romantic. Paris to Marseille. Not diesel and fiberglass."

Tracy looked at her daughter, then at the line of lights riding the Jersey shore like a necklace. "Romance is just logistics that work," she said. "We'll take logistics."

The bow rose and fell like a tired chest. The compass card held its steady slow whisper west of south. A freighter's horn rolled across them, deep as a cathedral.

"Sector New York, be advised—" a voice crackled on sixteen, some other drama playing out between Staten Island and the Kill, none of it theirs. They were just a sailboat headed south for the winter. That lie fit like a borrowed coat.

They cleared the last blink of the Verrazzano and felt the river loosen its grip. The ocean was a different animal—longer breath, wider shoulders. The boat seemed to notice and settle into it.

Vega glanced at the sky and read a line of cloud like a promise. He reached to the helm and clicked the autopilot, locking Mistral on a bearing that would carry her toward Sandy Hook, her AIS broadcasting a perfect, harmless story.

"Ellie," Tracy said quietly, all command now. "Lower the transom. Pull the tender. Mount the engine. Move."

Elle dropped her cup, already in motion. She hit the switch and the wide swim platform/transom hummed down, hinging to kiss the sea. The garage yawned open, revealing the boat's tender nested tight—no inflation needed—its small outboard secured beside it.

Whitman and Vega worked the lashings while Elle guided the tender out along its rails; Vega swung the outboard onto its bracket, tightened the clamps, primed the bulb.

"Everyone in," Tracy said.

Whitman stepped down first, steadying the bow line. Elle climbed in after him, then Vega. Tracy turned, grabbed a duffel from under the cockpit bench—heavy, zippered, anonymous—and dropped it into the tender before lowering herself over the transom and onto the gunwale.

"Push," she said.

Whitman shoved them clean. The tender slipped off the transom and dropped into Mistral's wake, the bigger boat's stern light painting the chop a faint, milky white. Tracy thumbed a remote in her pocket; the transom lifted obediently, sealing the garage with a soft hydraulic sigh until Mistral was again a sleek, closed animal slipping south under her own story.

They let the wake carry them. Within minutes, Mistral had disappeared into the dark, just another slow-moving constellation among buoys and freighters—a perfect decoy for any eye watching a screen.

Tracy leaned close as she tossed the transom's remote into the still dark sea. "Start it. Then ease north. Back to the city. Quietly."

Vega nodded, hit the starter; the tender's engine coughed, caught, and settled into a quiet mechanical purr. Whitman killed the running light. Vega turned the tiller and eased on power, threading the tender north through the Narrows along the Jersey side—low and dark—then into the Hudson's western seam, back toward New York City while, far astern, Mistral kept on being seen by all the right people.

By the time the Palisades loomed, the city glow was ahead of them again.

"That should buy us at least until dawn," Tracy said quietly.

Just after Dawn - Raven Rock

The bunker never slept. It hummed—a constant, arterial throb of servers, generators, air handlers. Fluorescents flattened faces into masks. Maps lived on screens, pulsing with colors that meant compliance or trouble.

"Recap," President Ted Hawley said.

A glass-walled conference cube filled behind him with silhouettes, each dragging a laptop and a private fear. Attorney General Mark Clark had a folder too thick for one night. Vice President Joe Harris hovered, sanctimonious and small. Chairman of the Joint Chiefs James Bragg sat very still. Speaker Michael McCollins dabbed his forehead with a linen handkerchief and practiced looking resolute.

"Rockefeller?" Hawley asked.

"Phones went dark," the operations lead said. "We had her convoy, but they split at Twenty-Third. The decoy ran north on the Taconic. We stopped them near Yorktown Heights— empty."

"How do you lose three SUVs?" Hawley's voice was soft and deadly.

"We didn't lose three," the lead said, palms up, like someone showing an empty bowl. "We lost one."

Clark slid a memo forward like a placemat. "We're expanding pulls from ALPRs on the West Side and FDR. Facial from traffic cams. Port Authority footage. Every feed within two miles of Rockefeller Center."

"What about the water?" Bragg asked, the first words he'd offered. "Ferries. Marinas."

"Already tasking Coast Guard and Harbor Patrol," the lead said. "AIS scrapes, VHF recordings. We'll cross-check hull IDs against... everything."

"Everything," Hawley repeated, liking the word. "Do it."

He pivoted, catching the aide with the wide eyes. "And find me a list of every pilot flying out of Teterboro, White Plains, and the heliports."

"Yes, sir."

Hawley looked to Bragg. "You, Harris, and McCollins will stand behind me," he said, not a question. "We address the nation again at 8:00 a.m."

Bragg's jaw moved once, as if he were testing a tooth. "I will, Mr. President."

"You can do more than that," Clark murmured. "Find Rockefeller and stabilize the situation."

McCollins found his courage in the echo of power. "The House stands with the President," he said, speaking as if into a camera already recording. "We will not allow—"

"Save it for your tape," Hawley cut in. "We're flooding the zone today."

He pointed at Communications. "I want the second address on every major outlet, 8 a.m. this morning. Cold open, no intro. Then we drop Bragg and McCollins' statements—no advance, no commentary. Let the morning news anchors figure it out."

"Sir," the comms director said, "we should soften the language—calm the markets, the cities, the suburbs. Lead with 'peace' and 'protect.' Then give them the Guard."

"Calm," Hawley repeated. "Peace. The Guard. Good." He smoothed his tie until it lay where it was supposed to. "Make me sound reasonable, responsible, caring—and like continuity."

They dressed the replica Oval Office the way undertakers dress the dead: careful, reverent, and convincingly sober. The portrait of Washington had been repositioned to sit in frame over Hawley's left shoulder. The flag stood nearer, so its gold fringe twinkled in the light.

Hawley walked in with Bragg, Harris, and McCollins waddling behind him like fat commas.

"General," Hawley said, under his breath, "we will not use the word 'federalize.'"

Bragg's eyes were the gray of old steel. "We will use 'support of civil authorities,'" he said.

"Fine," Hawley said. "But the effect will be the same."

He took his place behind the desk. The red light above the camera blinked alive. The prompter scrolled the first line like a priest making an offering.

"My fellow Americans," Hawley began, softer than earlier. "Today I ask for calm."

He let the word rest. Calm.

"There are those who would exploit uncertainty," he went on, "who would sow fear, who would turn disagreement into disorder. I have therefore asked our great nations' Governors to call out the National Guard in support of our civil authorities in major cities across our country—to secure voting counting sites, keep and restore order as needed and to ensure the peace. These are temporary measures, meant to protect our sacred elections."

Behind him, Bragg stood at rest, eyes forward, every ribbon on his chest an argument he did not make aloud. McCollins fixed his expression into grave solidarity. Harris looked small and insignificant. The shot framed them like pillars of state.

"We are one nation," Hawley said. "We will not be bullied by mobs, fouled by conspiracy theories, or misled by foreign actors. Go home. Let the process work. Trust the institutions designed by our founding fathers."

He did not say their names. He let the portrait over his shoulder do the work.

"Thank you," he finished, and the camera light died.

"Good," he said to nobody in particular. "Clip it for socials. Ten seconds. Twenty. Cut a forty-five."

The comms director's headset buzzed. "We'll push it all out at the top of the hour across the majors."

"Let's hear them," Hawley said.

Bragg's tape came up first: the General alone against a neutral backdrop, service dress immaculate. His voice was recited from the same muscle that had commanded troops for decades.

"As Chairman of the Joint Chiefs," Bragg said, "I affirm that our armed forces stand ready to support lawful civil authority as needed to preserve public safety and the integrity of our democratic process. We urge all Americans to remain calm, respect curfews where imposed, and allow state and local officials to do their duty. We will execute lawful orders and protect the nation."

Lawful. The word hung in the air like a life ring thrown to a drowning man who had not yet decided whether to catch it.

McCollins' tape followed: the Speaker in the Capitol's Statuary Hall, pre-recorded before the building locked down, flanked by bronzes of men whose names fewer citizens could remember with each passing year.

"The House of Representatives stands united behind the President's call for peace and order," he intoned. "We cannot allow chaos to undermine the election. We will work with our colleagues in the Senate to ensure continuity of government."

He had practiced *continuity* for an hour in a mirror.

"Good," Hawley said. "Let's get the message out."

On a dozen control-room walls across the country, producers loaded the latest announcements. Anchors with perfect hair read intros built from the White House feeds. Expert panels filled every network's newsroom. The words *secure vote counting sites, calm*, *order*, and *National Guard* slid into the bloodstream.

Across the Nation

Not everyone reacted the same way.

In Columbus, the governor said on live TV, "I see no reason to deploy the Ohio National Guard; you are ordered to remain in your barracks." In Austin, the governor said the opposite and tried to look like he had thought of it first. In Boise, a sheriff went on Facebook and declared he would not "harass citizens for trying to protect the ballot boxes."

Mid Morning - Raven Rock

In the bunker, the search unit had expanded to a second room with its own hum.

"We've got thirty-eight boats departing marinas from Yonkers to Bayonne within ninety minutes of the Rockefeller extraction window," an analyst said, pointing with a pen capped between her teeth. "AIS returns match twenty-seven. Eleven are dark."

"Profiles?" Hawley asked.

"Three are stronger possibilities," she said. "Beneteau Oceanis Yacht in Chelsea Pier logs, slip C-12. Name Mistral. Departure around the window. AIS pinged at the Battery; now headed south at eight knots. Could be them, could be winter traffic."

"Coast Guard?" Bragg asked.

"They can query and board under standing authority," the analyst said, "but we risk creating ten news stories before we find what we're looking for."

"Board them all," Hawley said.

Bragg did not move. "We don't stop boats without a predicate," he said, very quietly.

Hawley turned his head slowly, as if the general's voice were something in his teeth.

"Then we make sure it's them," Clark said quickly. "Get footage from Chelsea Piers. Look for agents, for the daughter. Cross with marina key fobs, garage cameras."

"Sir," another analyst cut in, "we have license plates on a box truck that took two cell phones north—it's odd. Pings stopped, then reappeared in motion on I-87, then vanished again. Looks like… dumped."

Hawley pointed at the screen with Mistral's slow bead ticking south. "Call Sector New York. Put eyes on that boat and the other two possibles. Quietly. I want a cutter shadowing and a helicopter high enough not to spook them."

Bragg didn't nod. He didn't have to; the captain in the corner was already typing.

Morning - North of Richmond

John Webster watched Hawley's second address from his living room in the Richmond suburbs, with the sound turned low and the captions turned on. He had taught himself years ago to distrust tone and listen to words.

His wife had gone to bed when the first address ran. She had said a prayer at the stairs for the country he had loved longer than he had loved his party. The house had that careful, creaky quiet old houses have at night.

Webster picked up his phone and stared at the contact labeled Chief Justice Anthony Hoyt. He didn't have to scroll; it was pinned fat and obvious. He tapped it.

Hoyt answered on the first ring. "John."

"Mr. Chief Justice," Webster said, defaulting to formality as the ground under him moved.

"Don't say anything else on this line," Hoyt said.

"Anthony—"

"Not a word," Hoyt repeated. "If you want to talk to me, come to my office. Now. And do so quietly."

Webster looked at the mantle clock. 8:45 a.m. "I can be there within two hours."

"Use a car you can forget," Hoyt said. "Leave your phone where it will be found later in the day. Bring no staff. If anyone asks, you're going to your hunting cabin."

The line went dead.

Webster put the phone down on the hall table beside his keys. Then he thought better of it. He left the phone on the kitchen counter with an old campaign coffee mug propped over it like a paperweight. It would dutifully ping the home Wi-Fi all day like a dog waiting at the door.

He pulled on a windbreaker too thin for the time of year. In the garage, he bypassed the armored SUV his staff preferred and slid behind the wheel of a clean 2008 Ford F-150 whose only luxury was heat. He turned the radio off, headlights to low, and rolled out as the sun rose toward the nation's capital.

Mid Morning - Raven Rock

Hawley watched Bragg's and McCollins' taped statements run on three networks at once. Overlays popped on the wall with sentiment analysis trailing hashtags and county-level heat maps that looked like a bad rash. The comms director said, "Positive with older demos, neutral with suburban women, angry in college towns." Markets in Asia twitched and settled.

"Let's cut a third address," Hawley said, We will run it early afternoon." "No more than 5 minutes, from the same desk. "Message to be, remain calm, trust the process, we will prevail.'"

"Yes, sir."

He waited until most of his people had drifted back to their banks of screens, then crooked a finger at Bragg. The general joined him in the fake Oval and closed the door.

"You looked good," Hawley said.

"I looked present," Bragg said.

"This only works if the uniforms stand where the camera can see them."

"It only works if the troops believe the orders are lawful," Bragg said, careful with each word, like a man stepping across ice of unknown thickness.

"We have the Attorney General," Hawley said, nodding toward Clark. "He can tell the troops what the law is."

"Opinions are not statutes," Bragg said. "We will not order soldiers to confront law-abiding citizens absent a lawful predicate."

Hawley's smile died and then revived, smaller. "I'm not asking you to order anything, James. I'm asking you to stand up and be seen."

"I did," Bragg said.

A long beat. Two men, one desk, a portrait.

"That's all, General," Hawley said finally.

Bragg left the room feeling more tired than he had in years. In the corridor, McCollins intercepted him, eyes glittering with the adrenaline of having been useful.

"We did what needed doing," the Speaker said, eager for affirmation.

Bragg looked at him as if he were a bird that had flown into the wrong room. He walked quickly past.

Mid Morning - Raven Rock & off the Jersey Shore

The analyst in the search room adjusted her glasses again and drew a line with her finger along the screen. "Mistral cleared the Narrows," she said. "Speed steady. Heading suggests Sandy Hook. A cutter out of Staten Island is shadowing from a mile and a half. Helo's high at six thousand. No chatter on sixteen. They indicated on the radio they were headed to Annapolis."

"Annapolis," Hawley repeated, savoring the coincidence as if names had power. "How long to Delaware Bay?"

"Eight hours at that speed," she said. "Maybe less if they ride the tide."

"Tell the cutter to hold distance," Bragg said from the doorway. He knew exactly why he said it. "We board in a couple of hours when the seas settle and the wind dies down."

Hawley didn't argue. This time there was no rush as they weren't going to be able to break surveillance.

He stepped back into the replica Oval. The portrait watched him again with its borrowed authority, patient and grave. He considered truer props—an open Bible, a pocket Constitution—and settled on nothing. Words would do.

"Get me the draft for the next address," he said, and the comms director nodded.

On one screen, the city glowed like an ember. On another, a little bead moved down the coast, stubborn and small. On a third, sentiment graphs climbed and dipped.

Mid Morning - I95

In the sea of traffic stretching from Richmond and Washington, John Webster drove north with the kind of concentration that leaves no room for fear. He thought about the sentence he would speak to Anthony Hoyt in a room that ought to be marble and might have to be a broom closet.

I won't be party to it, he would say. *Tell me what the law requires and I will stand there, even if I stand alone.*

He passed an unmarked cruiser tucked onto the shoulder. It did not move. He drove on, the road a ribbon, the future an unknown.

He crossed the Potomac alone. Fog rose from the water in sheets. He did not speed. Men who flee get caught. Men who drive like old law professors are invisible.

Morning - Raven Rock

Back underground, Hawley laced his fingers behind his head and closed his eyes, smiling to feel the whole machine turning because he had told it to. Above ground, in a city of domes and columns, a light was on in a private office where a Chief Justice waited for a visitor and a discussion he had hoped never to have.

Two Hours before Dawn -South Cove, NYC

The tender ghosted along the Battery's black edge, engine whispering, the skyline turning the river into a bowl of light. Vega kept them tight to the pilings where the shadows lived. South Cove opened like a small, deliberate bite taken out of the esplanade—curved stone, low rail, a pocket of water the city pretended was ornamental.

A man in a dark peacoat stood with his hands in his pockets, not looking at them. When the bow nosed the granite, he crouched and took the line without ceremony.

"George," Tracy said.

"Tracy," he returned, and then, for Elle, "Ms. Rockefeller." He said the name like an old New York aristocrat.

George Post had the kind of face that belonged to a building's cornerstone—weathered smooth, old chiseling that cut deep. His family had been New York real estate since before the American Revolution. Centuries worth of maps lived in his head; and even more were gathering dust in flat files in his office's basement.

"You're late," he said mildly.

"We took the scenic route," Tracy said.

"Of course you did." His eyes flicked to Vega and Whitman, scanned them once. "We don't have long."

They stepped off, handing up the duffel. The cold came off the stones chilling them. Post lifted the tender's painter and held it. He then reached under the gunwale and pulled a drain plug that wanted to stay put.

Vega understood before he asked. "You sure?"

Post didn't answer. He found the fuel-line clamp, closed it before putting two neat slits into each of the two pontoons. He dropped the tender and the current immediate pulled it back out into the Hudson. The tender began to settle. In less than a minute, there was nothing left to see.

"Walk," Post said.

They moved north along the esplanade with their heads down, a family late from dinner. Post guided them off the path at a hedge break nobody used and across a service lane to a set of steps the city had forgotten to mark.

"Phones?" Post asked without turning.

"Gone," Tracy said. "Earlier."

They cut inland through Battery Park City's clean geometry and then east, the air sharpening as the river fell away. Trinity Church rose in front of them like the city's conscience—spires and slate and the kind of quiet that has to be enforced. The gate to the yard stood on a tilt that pretended to be locked. Post pushed and it gave with a groan.

"Quickly," he said.

The church door opened on the nudge of a brass handle everyone assumed was decorative. Inside, the air was thick with history. The nave was dark except for a single votive flickering mid-aisle. Post led them along a side aisle to a small door that looked like a wall panel. A key turned in a slit in the rock that was virtually invisible.

"The camera that watched this went down in 2020," Post said. "Nobody cared enough to replace it."

Steps went down. Stone sweated. The crypt felt like something the city had forgotten about over a century ago. Post clicked a small light—no beam, just a glow like a cigarette cupped in a palm—and showed them a low room with three arched offshoots. Old names lived in brass. The floor pitched once and then settled.

"You'll be safe till morning," he said. "No one comes down here except the ghosts."

He handed Tracy a map, folded into a long, narrow rectangle, onion-skin thin and edged with the careful dirt of centuries. It was not a tourist's fantasy; it was utilities and vaults, hand-dug corridors, basement-to-basement cuts from the age before inspections. A red pencil line climbed from Trinity to a dozen possible shadows.

"Later today," Post said, tapping a crosshatched square near the edge, "At noon, here. Then we'll move you again."

Tracy didn't ask where *here* was, not now. She slid the map into her jacket and gripped his wrist, a thank-you that was more contract than sentiment.

Post looked at Elle, at Vega, at Whitman. "No lights if you can help it. No prayers out loud," he added with a smug grin. "I'll signal once in the morning before I come back. Two quick knocks followed by one and the word 'bond.' Anything else, you stay silent and leave via one of the tunnels on the map."

He backed up the steps; going the way he had arrived—without spectacle. The panel sighed shut. The church returned to its slumber.

In the small alcove off of the crypt, the silence broke, Elle said, "George Post. You never told me."

Tracy eased onto a stone bench. "Some friends are better kept quietly and at a distance." "They can help you more if they aren't caught up in the storm of your life."

Vega stood a while longer, head canted, ears searching the ceiling for the sound of feet. Whitman sat with his back to a pillar and finally let his shoulders drop.

"Get some sleep," Tracy said. "It will be a very long day." And then to no one in particular, "this really isn't where I envisioned spending my first night as President-Elect."

"How scared are you?" Elle asked finally.

Tracy thought about lying but there was far too much of that going on already.

"Very," she said. "Professionally terrified. Personally terrified. Also extremely annoyed."

Elle huffed a short laugh. "At whom?"

"At Hawley. At myself. At the people supporting him, At the Founders for not writing 'no narcissists' into the Constitution." Tracy shifted her back against the cold stone wall. "And mostly for dragging you into this."

"I volunteered," Elle said. "Remember."

Tracy softly said, "This isn't what you signed up for."

"Life sometimes takes different turns" Elle whispered back. "I came to you asking to be part of the campaign. I wrote half your economic talking points. I'm invested in this as much as you are."

For a moment, the only sound was Whitman snoring and a faint drip coming from the back of the crypt.

"I keep thinking about 2020," Elle said suddenly. "I was a kid, but I remember you saying, *The system bent, but it didn't break.* At the end of the day, the guardrails worked. I have faith that they will again."

Tracy closed her eyes briefly. "This feels like those rails have taken their hardest whack yet, I just hope they hold."

Elle paused and finally asked. "If they catch you, what do you want me to do?"

"If they catch me," she said, "you keep going. Tell the world about what happened. You don't let them twist this into some self-serving conspiracy theory."

Elle laughed then the weight of the situation returned. "I'm angry," she said. "At him. At everyone who enabled him. At how easily this all slid sideways."

After a while, Tracy reached across and took her hand. "Now get some sleep," she said. "Tomorrow is going to be another long intense day."

Late Morning - Washington D.C.

John Webster stepped through the Supreme Court's side entrance and thought absurdly about how often he had visited the building as a young lawyer just to feel small on purpose. Today the smallness was all encompassing.

Anthony Hoyt's door was ajar. The Chief Justice sat behind the desk with his hands folded, a statue of self-control. He glanced up once, met Webster's eyes, and tapped two fingers on the blotter—silence.

A shadow moved behind the bookcases. Associate Justice Walter Lockwood stepped into the light and made a small tilt of the head that meant *come*.

Webster followed Lockwood through a staff corridor that smelled faintly of paper and lemon oil, down a service stairwell whose steps had known the soles of janitors and night clerks, and into the basement. Lockwood used a keycard, then a key, then something that was neither. A door marked MECHANICAL swung in heavily on its hinges.

Beyond lay a tunnel the public had never seen—part utility, part legacy, a right-of-way from a renovation long ago. The air was cool and still. Lockwood didn't turn on the lights; he knew every joint and jog.

"Cameras?" Webster whispered, breaking Hoyt's earlier instruction because the question was of utmost concern.

"Not down here," Lockwood said. "And nowhere on Supreme Court Property"

They walked for what felt like several blocks before finally reaching a steel door without a label, Lockwood paused, listened, and pushed. They came up in an alley where nothing watched—no domes on poles, no black irises under eaves.

"Two blocks more," Lockwood murmured.

They moved like men of no consequence. A turn, then another, and then the brass knocker of a nondescript Georgetown townhouse that no one ever gave a second glance to.

Lockwood gave three small raps. The door opened on Harry Bell's face, his expression the calm of a banker who had seen more than his fair share of crises.

"Inside," Bell said. "Quickly."

The boardroom lights were low. At the center of the table sat a single object: a sealed letter on creamy vellum, addressed in George Washington's hand—not a copy, not a transcription—to "The Leader of the Senate."

Webster stopped as if he had seen a ghost. He recognized the handwriting. Washington.

Lockwood nodded to the envelope. *Open it.*

Webster's fingers weren't quite steady. The wax cracked with a sound that made time feel thin. He unfolded the sheet and read. The script was elegant.

"*Sir,*

When a faction threatens our Republic, the Senate's first duty is to ensure the peaceable execution of the Constitution. In such an hour, you are commanded to steady your chamber, acknowledge the lawful returns, and join with the House to deny any pretender's powers. Let no man—ever—set aside the citizens' vote. You will work under the direction of the Guarantors, whom I and your forebears have charged to be the ultimate guardians of the Constitution and the great American experiment.

There was more, much more which explained who the 13 Guarantors were and the power they could yield. Webster read it twice and then lowered the page.

"He wrote it to me," Webster said, meaning *to my office*, for this *moment*.

"He wrote it for you," Hoyt said from the doorway, having followed in silence. "And for any man who inherits your seat of power.

Webster exhaled the way a diver exhales who ran out of air ten feet down and has just now breached the surface.

Lockwood took the seat beside Webster with the intimacy of a co-conspirator. "You should stay here for the rest of the evening." "We will discuss next steps in the morning when we know more about what Hawley has planned."

Webster looked at the vellum again. The Leader of the Senate written in Washington's hand. He now knew the burden Prometheus carried.

Bell interjected, I am going to leave you to fully absorb the weight of the contents. We have a room for you to use while here, Lockwood will show you to it.

Late Morning - Off the Jersey Shore

The sea was a sheet of cold dark rolling anger under a sky that had not yet decided to be blue. A Coast Guard cutter hunted its prey. Belowdecks, a faint scorch was visible along the engine bay bulkhead—heat without open flame. In a forward locker, a sealed drybag held a wallet card and monogrammed items belonging to Tracy Rockefeller and Elle; the bag was intact and dry when logged.

"Mistral, this is Coast Guard cutter *Shearwater*. Prepare to be boarded."

Mistral did not answer. She held her eight knots.

The boarding team came over the rail in three practiced movements: hook, heel, swing. Boots found fiberglass with the certainty of a hundred drills. A young petty officer swept the cockpit with a flashlight he didn't need.

"Sector, boarding party on," a voice said, bored and precise. "No souls visible topside."

The autopilot blinked its small, contented blink. Two cups rode in their holders, cold coffee long past pleasant. A thermos lay on its side against the companionway lip, rattling when the boat's shoulders moved.

"Down below," the coxswain said.

The cabin smelled faintly of coffee and salt and the metal smell of a wrench used recently. A locker held life jackets that had been counted and recounted. The tender garage was shut and latched. A pair of wet footprints, faint as intentions, paraded from the companionway to the aft head and faded.

"Sector, we have signs of recent activity," the petty officer reported. "No persons aboard."

"Confirm tender status," a voice crackled back.

The coxswain glanced at the transom controls and found the manual overrides. "Tender missing," he said. "And when were they closest to the Jersey shore?"

The helmsman, still on the cutter, answered from the chart table. "About 0300 near Long Beach Island.

A pause long enough to matter.

"Copy," the voice said at last. "Search the boat again. Bag anything you find. Then log its track and then put it under tow.

"Aye."

In a cold control room dug deep below Raven Rock, the screens watched a boat now stopped. In the gray light, the cutter's boarding team moved like men cleaning up after a party they hadn't been invited to.

They would find nothing. They would write it down anyway. And in a church crypt surrounded by centuries of bones, four people tried to get a few hours' sleep.

11:00 a.m. - Trinity Crypt - NYC

They'd slept in shifts on the cold stone. Whitman posted himself by the alcove entrance, Vega kept one palm resting on the duffel as if it were a dog that might bolt, and Tracy slept with her back pressed to an old brass nameplate. Elle, wrapped in a scratchy borrowed wool, somehow looked the most comfortable of the four.

Right before 11 a.m., the mechanical alarm in Tracy's beautiful Patek sang its discreet chime—an old Christmas present from her long-divorced husband and Elle's father. Tracy came awake in one movement and nudged the others.

"We need to move now," she said, voice low but decisive. "According to George's map, it'll take us an hour to reach the noon meeting point."

She opened the duffel and pulled out knit caps, sunglasses, and a handful of energy bars, passing them around. Whitman added the field rules, as if reciting a drill, they all knew but needed to hear again. "Heads down if we're on the street, no eye contact, walk with pace and purpose," he said. "We spread out, but everyone stays within sight. If one of us gets picked up or spotted, the others keep going."

In the top-left corner of the map, George had written in his neat engineer's hand: *start at Bleecker, follow the light and go right on red.* Tracy turned the sheet so everyone could see. "We need the Bleecker vault," she said. "That's our way out."

By the glow of the dim LED George had left for them, they worked deeper into the crypt, reading names, breathing dust. Far back on the left they finally found it: BLEECKER, an iron gate rusted to a dull brown. Whitman shoved; the gate gave with a ragged sigh. The little chamber beyond was damp and close and felt like it remembered everything.

"Follow the light?" Elle whispered.

"Kill the LED," Tracy said.

Darkness wrapped them—and in it, a faint line of light revealed itself at the back wall, seeping through a thin crack between two marble slabs.

Tracy nodded once to Whitman, toward the seam. "Push."

With a steady shove, the slab pivoted on a hidden pin and swung inward, revealing a tight, dimly lit passage that snaked away from the church. One by one they climbed through. Whitman leaned back and, with a careful pull, eased the slab back into place until it softly kissed the jamb.

To the group Tracy said quietly, "when the tunnel splits, look for something marked in red, then take the path just to the right of it. That should carry us to George."

They moved into the maze.

Late Afternoon - The Townhouse

The air in the boardroom was heavy; the smell of coffee had settled into the old wood. The beech box still sat in the center of the table where it had been since midnight; the little pewter bell charm lay beside it, mute but present. Everyone looked as like they had slept with the weight of the world tormenting their dreams.

All thirteen were present, plus Chief Justice Hoyt. No one bothered with small talk. Bell started simply.

"We have the authority," he said, giving the matter the weight it deserved, "and we have the instruments to implement that authority. What we don't have yet is enough information on Hawley's intentions to build an effective plan. So: no overt action today—unless we use our two governors to push back publicly if his next moves demand it." He let his gaze move around the table. "We let Hawley play his cards while we put our pieces in place. Agreed?"

Nods circled the room.

Rhode Island—John Teruel—set a brushed-aluminum case on the table, flipped two latches, and opened it like a small stage. Inside lay fourteen matte-black handsets with stubby antennas, no logos, each nested in foam.

"When I ran Lockheed," he said, almost casual, "we built a system—just for us. Records of its existence were destroyed. It rides a buried receiver in an old weather satellite. These only connect to each other. Fourteen channels are already mapped in our usual order: New Hampshire is One; the Chief Justice is Fourteen."

He looked around. "Pick one up. Press the little red button on top. Hold the front up to your face until it chirps."

Chirps hopped around the table one by one.

"Good," Teruel said. "Iris-locked. We also have untraceable comms to the outside world, in place—in both locations."

Bell turned to New Hampshire—Senator Susan Lewis—who hadn't taken her eyes off the box and the phones. "You went to Dartmouth with Tracy," he said, gentling the request.

"Any idea where she might be? Anyone we can trust to find her? Can you quietly put out feelers?"

"I don't but someone we went to school with might," Lewis said. "George Post, I don't dare call. It will have to be done in person. I will head to New York City as soon as we finish."

"Good," Bell said. "Let me know what you find—on these only."

Bell then placed both hands on the table. "Washington understood better than anyone that you never put your eggs all in one basket. As such, he made provisions for a 2nd base for the Guarantors, the Lodge, buried deep within his extensive Ohio River Valley landholdings. Virginia (Bill McLean) knows its location and has been its custodian since the beginning. Virginia, please take Georgia, New Jersey, Maryland, North Carolina, South Carolina to the Lodge. The Lodge has state of the art, secure, broadcast facilities, which we may need to use in the coming days. I'd suggest you go in two groups and please do so as anonymously as possible. Teruel's handsets can be used to help guide you. McLean, you will then need to get back to your state's capital. Delaware, you will need to get to Springfield as well. When you both arrive, please issue public statements ordering your National Guard troops to remain in their barracks. This will further increase the pressure on Hawley." The Lodge maintains redundant power and a hardened uplink for broadcast.

"When you get to the lodge, Georgia -Lynn Tyler – please reach out to your network and see if we can set up peaceful marches in major cities in support of counting the vote. When they are ready let me know and we can agree timing."

"One more request before you'll head out, North Carolina - George Damon – we need a favor from our closest friend. Please call wife's uncle, the King of England. Ask him to get his Prime Minister to deliver a message to the Chinese and Russians for us......they are to stay out of it. Any attempts to interfere will be viewed very dimly."

Bell looked to the doorway. "Before we disperse—Senator Webster."

John Webster stepped in, tie a little off, eyes showing the stress he was under. Hoyt gave a small nod toward the hearth chair; Webster sat.

"John," Bell said, "I want you to stay here tonight. No calls. No messages. We're going to let Hawley overplay his hand, then we'll begin to rein him in. When it's time, we'll need you to deliver the Senate."

Webster touched the inside pocket where Washington's vellum letter rode and nodded. "I'll be ready."

"Good," Bell said. "We'll need you."

"Rhode Island?" Bell added.

Teruel pulled a large duffel onto the table and unzipped it to reveal rows of boxed iPhones. "Burners," he said. "Take several. Use once. Destroy."

Chairs scraped softly as the Guarantors rose, pocketed handsets and burners, and left the room. The last two in the boardroom were Bell and Hoyt.

"Harry," Hoyt said, low, "I'm worried about Webster. I'm not sure he'll hold under this."

"I know," Bell said. "But he truly despises Hawley and he's a firm believer in the Constitution. He needs time to get his head around what's in front of him."

Hoyt nodded. "I'm heading back to the Court. I asked Massachusetts to come with me. It's likely going to be a long night."

Noon - Raven Rock

You could almost taste the bunker's air—stale, thick, and a little sweet.

"Rockefeller?" Hawley asked without looking up.

"Nothing," the ops lead said. "The boat was a ghost. Mistral was empty when boarded. Signs of recent activity, tender missing, track suggests a break near the Jersey shore around oh-three-hundred. We're sweeping cameras along the Hudson and Jersey shore. We're also—"

"Just find out where she went," Hawley said.

Feeds crowded a wall: shaky phone video from a shut-down counting center in Ohio where a sheriff stood in a doorway like a reluctant usher; a press conference in Phoenix where a county recorder refused to close the doors; an Ohio governor whose jaw said no with conviction and no trace of fear; a Texas adjutant general standing beside a podium with a seal and three flags.

"…support to civil authorities," he was saying, "to ensure safety around ballot-counting sites as directed by the governor. These are precautionary deployments."

In Wisconsin, a county canvassing board stacked pizza boxes and then kept counting ballots. In Nevada, a clerk cried quietly into a sleeve off-camera and then checked another signature.

"The states are fragmenting," the comms director said softly, almost to herself.

"We're asserting," Hawley said, not softly. "Then we consolidate. The difference is who wins."

Bragg stood in the doorway. He didn't sit. "Mr. President, I need five minutes."

Hawley steered him into the replica Oval and shut the door.

"Update me," Hawley said.

"I tried General Charles Taylor," Bragg said. "Northern Command. Wanted his posture if we declare an insurrection."

"And?"

"He didn't pick up," Bragg said. "Which is its own answer."

"Try again."

Bragg did. The line hummed, then connected on the second ring.

"James," Taylor said. No rank. No sir.

"Charles," Bragg said. He kept his voice flat. "If I get a request from the President to take action against a possible insurrection, what would Northern Commands position be?"

"There would have to be a lawful predicate," Taylor said. "Which, for the record, the President doesn't currently have."

Bragg felt the old ache in the shoulder that remembered a fall down a mountain he'd insisted wasn't there. "This is open to interpretation," he said.

"Soldiers need certainty and clarity," Taylor said. "James, if you ask a platoon to do a thing they think is illegal, they simply will not. You might get different answers to the same question at different bases, but if you do, that should be enough to tell you its not right. When something is right, the answer is clear."

"On the ops-room wall beyond the door, a red banner cut across a live feed: POLLING STATION FIRE EXCHANGE — OKLAHOMA COUNTY. Sound came up too hot, then steadied. Two men ducked behind folding tables. Someone yelled, "Cease fire! Cease—" The frame froze, jumped, returned at a new angle. A red pickup fishtailed in gravel; a deputy's hat lay upside down in the rain.

Bragg closed his eyes once. "We'll speak later, Charles."

"I expect we will," Taylor said, and hung up.

Hawley stared at the frozen image. "Find Rockefeller," he said without moving his lips, "and a list of governors we can count on."

He stepped back into the hum. "Next announcement at one," he told comms. "Thirty seconds. Calm. Restraint. We need to look like we are in complete control."

In a far corner, Jimmy Walsh sat at a console staring at a screen. He didn't entirely understand everything going on but it didn't feel right. Whatever was happening, it was increasingly making him feel uncomfortable.

11:45 a.m. - The Tunnel - NYC

After what felt like an eternity of dim bulbs and brick, the passage ended at a single industrial steel door. Whitman tried the push bar. It opened onto a small wood-paneled room with no visible entrance or exit except the way they'd come. Daylight fell through a square skylight. In the middle stood a plastic folding table and four chairs. A picnic basket and four thermoses waited there as neatly as a welcome.

"George was always a gentleman," Tracy said.

Her Patek read 11:45. "We've got a few minutes," she added. "Let's eat."

While she poured coffee, Elle asked, "Mom, what's the plan?"

Tracy paused with the thermos mid-tilt, the question hanging between them. "First, I need to know what's actually happening out there," she said at last. "Then who we can trust. Once I know those two things, I can speak to the country. Right now, the only things we know for sure are that Hawley is trying to slow or stop the vote count—and that the men who arrived at Rockefeller Center weren't coming to congratulate me."

Whitman nodded, let his shoulders drop against the paneling. Vega stretched his legs and sipped the still warm coffee. Tracy looked up at the square of sky and tried to picture what the rest of the day would hold.

12:30 p.m. - Raven Rock

With the next set of orders sent, Hawley walked past his own suite and went straight to the Vice President's. Raven Rock's VIP wing felt like a luxury hotel, just buried hundreds of feet underground—soft carpets, heavy doors, and no outside.

He didn't bother to knock. He opened the outer door and went straight to the bedroom, flicking on the lights.

Joe Harris jolted upright, a young aide, perched on top of him.

"Out," Hawley said. As she scrambled for her clothes and fled, eyes wide.

When the door shut, Hawley stared down at Harris. "Joe, do you ever give it a rest?" he said, not waiting for an answer. "I need you to do something this afternoon—and not get caught doing it. Reach out to the militias your people flirt with. Tell them our democracy is under threat, and their President needs their help now. Tell them to watch for traitors and do what's necessary."

Harris swallowed. "And if anyone asks who told me to—"

"No one will," Hawley said. "But if they do, you prayed on it."

He turned off the light on his way out, leaving Harris in darkness, like his soul.

Noon - Tunnel Holding Room

Precisely at noon: two quick knocks, a beat, one more, then the word "bond."

Tracy counted her breath, then nodded to Whitman. He eased the door an inch, then two. George Post's face appeared—smiling, tired, concerned.

"I've got a van upstairs. Heads down," he said, stepping in. "Friend's place at 993 Fifth— entire twelfth floor, owners away. Two entrances, both on camera. If you have to bolt, there's a one-way tunnel from the building's basement into an old Met storage room. Both doors will be unsecured for the next several days, however, if you do go though, they will lock automatically behind you."

"Move," Tracy said.

They climbed a single service stair. A plain white van idled on the loading dock, rear doors open. Post slid into the driver's seat, baseball cap low. Whitman shut them in. The van nosed into traffic.

Twenty minutes later they turned off Madison to East 81st, ducked into a townhouse garage, door closing behind them like a wink. They crossed a service passage to 993's rear entrance. A keyed freight car took them straight to 12. No witnesses, with no one the wiser as to who the new temporary residents of one of NYC's premier buildings happened to be.

Post walked them through the apartment—well-stocked larder, laptops, wifi, security camera coverage on the landings. At the door he pressed a single phone into Tracy's palm. "Only I have this number. Call if you need anything. I'll be back at noon tomorrow. Same signal."

The door clicked. Silence returned.

Early Evening - The Townhouse

Once everyone who was leaving was gone, Bell headed back to the pantry to get a quick bite to eat. The one thing the townhouse always had was a well-stocked pantry. He pulled a couple of pieces of sourdough bread out of a box, then threw a few slices of ham on top. He wasn't hungry but knew he needed to put something in his stomach if he had a hope of getting any sleep tonight. As he was about to take his first bite, Pennsylvania (General Charles Taylor) walked in. As it was just the two of them, all formality was immediately dumped.

"Charles," Harry said, as he handed over the centuries-old vellum written in Washington's hand—To the Commanding Officer — United States Army. "As Commander of U.S. Northern Command (NORTHCOM), you hold combatant command for the continental defense mission. Bragg outranks you, but absent a lawful predicate he cannot exercise operational authority on U.S. soil. What matters for us now is operational control inside the law. This letter should be in your hands. I'll let you decide if you need to show it to him at some point in the future. I don't think Bragg's a bad man; I just think he is somehow compromised."

Taylor slid the letter into his dress uniform's inner pocket.

"Thanks, Harry," Charles said. "I know the contents by heart, so I'll read it again quietly later. What is your next move?"

"Charles, if you want to destabilize a rich, self-absorbed, narcissistic egomaniac, you start by making him poor," Harry said. "Over the last several months, I've been quietly buying up all of his family oil company's debt. Most of the loans are callable if oil prices drop under sixty dollars a barrel. Both Amarco and Exxon are going to announce major new reserve discoveries tomorrow morning. That should push prices well under sixty. When that happens, we are calling the loans. Under the loan terms, he's only got three days to settle and we know Hawley doesn't have the cash to cover any of it. That will push the Hawley businesses into bankruptcy, and he is going to panic. It's all being done via an offshore shell company, Mount Vernon LLC, that's buried in a nest of other shell companies. He's going to have a very hard time reacting."

"Harry," Charles replied, "remind me to keep on your good side. I'm going to head down to Norfolk Naval Station. It will be easier for me to monitor developments from there, as it falls under my command." It's also got a standing JAG unit and secure comms.

Mid-Afternoon – Raven Rock

Vice President Harris slowly made his way out of the bunker and up to the surface. As he couldn't be seen leaving, he avoided the elevator and climbed the twenty miserable flights of stairs. He pushed up a small metal hatch. Once outside, he flipped on his personal cell phone and made three short calls to three militia leaders. The message was the same on each call: the Constitution is under threat; radicals and foreign actors are trying to seize power; your President needs your help. Within hours all three groups had mobilized their followers. Harris pointed the first group at Los Angeles, the second at Chicago, and the last was given Washington, D.C., as its target. Two more calls then followed to pastors who lived for the TV camera. The message was only slightly different: radicals and foreign actors are trying to seize power—please help us secure voting stations.

Calls completed, Harris snapped it back off, turned and began the descent back into his own private hell.

Evening – NYC Penn Station

Just after ten, New Hampshire—Senator Susan Lewis—stepped off the Acela. In a quiet corridor she dialed.

"Senator Lewis," Post said, warmly as they had been lovers once.

"George," she answered warmly. "We need to talk."

"Breakfast. Seven," Post said. An address arrived on her screen followed by a four-digit code for an elevator

Outside, she found a cab and gave the driver an Upper East Side boutique hotel that didn't exist unless you already knew it did.

Evening – Raven Rock

Hawley stepped back into the replica Oval for one last time today. The portraits on the wall behind him watched again and bestowed borrowed authority. The red recording light flicked on and the teleprompter started to roll. On the screen the words:

Request all Governors: mobilize National Guard troops to protect all polling and vote-counting stations. Vote counting remains suspended until further notice to prevent further unrest and looting by radical and foreign actors. Nationwide curfew from 8 p.m. to 6 a.m. starting tomorrow.

Within five minutes it was done. Hawley stood up, turned to the head of Comms, and stated, "Get it out on all the majors at nine p.m. tonight."

And with that he left for his private quarters for the night, feeling secure in his perceived position of control.

Evening – The Townhouse

Sitting on his bed in his private quarters in the sub-basement of the townhouse, Bell watched Hawley's 9 p.m. addresses. To a portrait of Washington hung on the wall, he muttered, tomorrow is going to be a long day for all of us. As he stood up to go turn off the lights for the night, the screen lit up on Teruel's secure handset. Two messages: Have arrived at the Lodge. All is Quiet. Followed by King is informed, messages will be delivered to the bear and dragon.

Day 3 – Heat Rises

Morning - Across America

The grid of screens was filled with talking and screaming heads.

Austin — the governor, with his adjutant general beside him: the Texas Guard would deploy "in support of civil authorities at counting centers."

Columbus — "Ohio Guard remains in the barracks," the governor said. "We have police for civil law enforcement."

Madison / Lansing / Richmond — Democratic governors stepped to podiums in front of flags chosen on purpose. "We will not enforce a federal curfew of dubious legality," Michigan's governor said. "We are filing for an injunction in federal court this morning."

Atlanta / Phoenix / Philadelphia / Toledo — crowds coagulated: handmade signs, cheap megaphones, folding chairs for the old. Pro-Hawley chants braided with anti-Hawley hymns. Deputies tried to separate the camps. In places, pastors prayed into cameras; in others, water bottles flew, and tempers grew exceedingly short.

Mid Morning - Raven Rock

The banners at the bottom of the screens in the control room scrolled tirelessly. Each of the screens on the left was tuned to a different major network. Fox was the first to pick it up. First, Amarco announced a major new reserve discovery in shallow waters near Jeddah in the Red Sea. Half an hour later, Exxon announced it had found a major new oil field in eastern Montana that would increase its proven reserves by close to 30%. The impact on the market was nearly immediate. With each trade, the benchmark Brent crude seemed to drop by another quarter-dollar. It had opened the day at $65.25 a barrel; by 10:30 a.m. it was down to $58.75.

At 11:15 a.m., the CFO of Hawley Oil, Nick Dolan, received an email from Mount Vernon LLC, a firm he had never heard of, with an address in Cyprus. Subject: **Notice of Acceleration — Hawley Oil Holdings.** Nick opened and scanned the email quickly. Several words at the bottom caught his eye: "settlement due in three days, settlement account details to follow on that day." Oil had dropped below $60 and the loans were being called. He uttered one word: "Fuck." He knew they were now badly exposed.

Dolan pulled out his phone and dialed the number of the man who had put him in this position. Hawley answered immediately.

"Acceleration, three billion in total?" Hawley said softly. "Three days to settle? I thought we took out all loans from First Republic Bank of Texas."

"We did," replied Dolan, "but they must have offloaded them. In fact, they've probably changed hands multiple times by now."

"Callable below sixty," Hawley said again, staring at Fox's ticker, before saying, "Do nothing," and then hanging up abruptly on Dolan.

"Get me Treasury," Hawley shouted to the nearest aide.

The Treasury Secretary, John Cohen, came on with a voice like an investment banker about to talk you into a trade completely against your interests. "Good morning, Mr. President."

"We have a problem, Mr. Secretary. I'm being targeted and I need you to find out by whom and why. They are trying to bankrupt Hawley Oil," Hawley yelled into his cell phone. "You need to stop it."

"Mr. President," Cohen replied, "this appears to be a private matter between two parties. I'm not sure it's our place to get involved. We can try to trace where the funds go if Hawley Oil makes a redemption, but that's about it. What I can do is see if a 'friendly firm' can offer Hawley Oil a bridge loan."

For the second time in five minutes, Hawley hung up abruptly.

Hawley looked over at Attorney General Clark. "Order them."

"Sir—"

"Order them," yelled Hawley.

Clark didn't move. "Order what?"

"Open a formal investigation into this Mount Vernon ghost. Beneficial owners, wires, other shells. I want to know everything there is to know about them by tonight," Hawley said, the words knifing through the room.

"On it," Clark said, before he scurried out of the room to call his chief aides.

The room was now empty. Hawley sat alone, a prisoner of his own insecurities.

The portrait of Washington watched him, judging his every thought.

"You had it easy," Hawley said under his breath.

In the reflection of one of the monitors, he saw himself at his most vulnerable, An old man in a fake office under a mountain, lit by LEDs. Then he imagined the way his enemies would tell the story if they prevailed.

He tried to steal it.

Ted Hawley, who couldn't let go. Ted Hawley, who turned the Guard on his own people. Ted Hawley, who lost the plot, the country, and then Presidency.

He closed his eyes, just once. The image didn't go away.

You can stop this now, some small, dim weak voice suggested. Concede. Call her. Say the right words. Walk out on January twentieth and let them clap.

He pictured Rockefeller's face. Hand on the bible taking the oath of office. Hawley sitting there watching as his world was ripped away.

He opened his eyes again. The lesson his grandfather had pounded into him the dining room table came back with crystal clarity: *If you show weakness, they will hang you with it.*

This wasn't about ego, he told himself. This was about survival, his. The brief moment of doubt evaporated.

Late Morning - Supreme Court - Washington, D.C.

Hoyt read the emergency filings like a tired professor facing a tower of uninspired term papers that all needed grading.

Michigan, Wisconsin, Pennsylvania: enjoin the federal curfew as ultra vires. Nevada, Arizona, Massachusetts: the vote count suspension violates the Elections Clause and state authority.

He initialed the routing sheet. "Set up an emergency conference of the full Court at 3 p.m.," he told the clerk. "Draft an emergency administrative stay on any federal directive that impedes the tallying of lawfully cast ballots. Make sure it's narrow, and state that the full Court will give it further review shortly. Do the same for Hawley's curfew. I want them both out before the 3 p.m. conference. Work with Lockwood on it." The clerk swallowed. "Yes, Chief." He looked at Lockwood. "This will definitely generate a reaction."

Late Morning - Raven Rock

Hawley grabbed Clark and pulled him into the corner. "I need you to get on the air and tell the nation we are going to push back hard on these governors who are challenging my authority. Then I need you and your best people back in D.C. and in front of the Supreme Court by tomorrow morning. Set up a private meeting with Hoyt and squeeze him hard. We need to make sure the Supreme Court doesn't become an impediment—and let Hoyt know that if he thinks he can, he will live to regret it."

Clark then grabbed the comms aide. "I need to tape a short piece ASAP pushing back on the governors who are challenging us on freezing the vote, deploying the National Guard, and the curfew. Make them out to be left-wing radicals."

The banks of screens across the back wall now showed:

Prince William County, VA — the Mountain Men militia mustered in a gravel lot behind a shuttered discount department store. Confederate flags fluttered from battered old pickup trucks. One group had set up a barbecue pit and was roasting a pig.

Cook County, IL — the Prairie Patriots had taken over a Walmart parking lot. Their leader was busy giving speeches while live-streaming himself. "We are here to defend democracy," he repeated over and over again.

And at vote-counting sites across the nation, "pro count" and "stop the steal" crowds were facing off, local sheriffs trying desperately to keep the two sides apart. So far it had been mostly peaceful, but temperatures were rising.

7:00 a.m. - Upper East Side - NYC

Lewis knocked on the front door of Post's brownstone on 18 E 64th Street at 7 a.m. on the dot. Post ushered her straight through to the garden in the back, where he had laid out a simple breakfast of coffee and pastries.

"It's safe to talk here, Susan. I know this isn't just a courtesy call," said Post.

"George, I need your help. I need to find Tracy and I'm guessing if anyone knows where she is, it's you," replied Lewis, before adding, "I'm here to help her."

Post smiled, sipped his coffee, and then subtly nodded his head.

"After breakfast," Post said. "We go together."

Lewis smiled and nodded—message sent, message received.

"Now, Susan, how have you been? It's been too long. Let's have a proper catch-up," finished Post.

12:00 p.m. - Raven Rock

Clark entered the fake Oval and signaled to clear the room. Once it was clear he turned to Hawley and said, "So far, nothing on Mount Vernon. We're continuing to dig, but so far we're just chasing shells companies."

Hawley stared at Clark, seething. "Keep looking and lean on our friends to help."

He followed with, "Any word on Rockefeller? She's likely trying to get to D.C., hoping she has

90

friends in Congress that can help her. Do we have eyes on all traffic heading south from New Jersey?"

"We do," replied Clark. "Right now, though, she's still a ghost."

"That's the best idea you've had in months!" blurted Hawley. "Now let's make her a ghost— which might just smoke her out. Get a release out to all the newswires. Say the Coast Guard recovered a sailboat, Mistral, registered to a foundation controlled by Tracy Rockefeller, adrift off New Jersey with signs of an engine fire. Note that belongings of Tracy Rockefeller and her daughter, Elle, were aboard. Mention we are treating it as a missing-persons case, but both are feared dead and lost at sea. No SOS was received."

"Smoke her out," Hawley said. "Get that out immediately. And find me her VP running mate, Chris Bolton. Get him here ASAP."

12:00 p.m. - 993 Fifth Ave - NYC

The elevator opened onto the entire twelfth floor. The front door leading into the apartment would normally be open, but today it was closed. Post stepped forward—two quick knocks, a beat, one more—then the word "bond." With that, Elle opened the door and ushered them in. As she did, she shot a look at Post. Post picked up on it immediately, stopped, and introduced her to the Senator, saying, "Elle, I'd like you to meet Susan Lewis. She's an old friend of both your mother's and mine from Dartmouth."

"George," Elle said, "I've met the Senator, but why is she here?"

Before Post could answer, Lewis replied, "I'm here to help. I'll explain when we sit down with your mother."

Elle led Lewis and Post through the living room to a private office off to the left. Vega and Whitman were perched right outside the door like two sentries. In the office, at the desk, Tracy sat staring in disbelief at a computer screen.

"George," Tracy said. Then: "Senator." Formal, but warm.

As they sat down, a news banner popped up on the computer screen:

Breaking News — The Mistral

US COAST GUARD: SAILBOAT *MISTRAL* FOUND ADRIFT OFF NEW JERSEY; BELONGINGS OF TRACY ROCKEFELLER & DAUGHTER ELLE RECOVERED; BOTH FEARED DEAD AND LOST AT SEA; NO SOS RECEIVED

Lewis was the first to speak. "Tracy, Hawley is trying to force you out into the open. We need to move you to a more secure location."

Tracy replied, "This feels very secure. Other than George, no one has any idea we're here."

Lewis pushed back. "It is—until it isn't. I found George, and they will eventually hone in on him as well. At best, you'll be cut off here and isolated. I have people and resources that can protect you and Elle while providing a platform from which to push back on Hawley. I just need you to trust me right now."

Tracy answered, "Before I say yes, I need to know what the plan is and who else is involved."

Lewis then pulled out the secure handset that Teruel had provided. Turning to the group, Lewis stated, "This is untraceable. Do you mind if I place a call?"

Shortly After Noon - Raven Rock

Bragg found a quiet corner between the living quarters and dining area. He pulled out his phone and dialed General Charles Taylor.

"Charles," he said when Taylor picked up—no rank, just two old warriors.

"James."

"I need to know where you stand."

"Ready to defend the Constitution, same as always," Taylor said.

"We should speak in person," stated Bragg.

"Agreed," Taylor said. "How about on the terrace by the Hudson—West Point, 1700 today. It'll give me an excuse to get a few flight hours in; I'm still trying to keep my wings."

Bragg closed his eyes a moment. "I'll be there."

Early Afternoon - Townhouse

It had been a quiet day so far at the townhouse for Bell. Shortly after 7 a.m., he received a message from Lewis that Post would take her to see Rockefeller. After breakfast with a still-shaken Webster, he settled down to monitor events when the secure handset rang. It was Taylor. Taylor quickly briefed him on the call with Bragg and indicated he would fly up to West Point in a Black Hawk helicopter with two Apaches for escort. Taylor assured Bell the crews were all people he would trust with his life. Bell then told Taylor that it was his call if and when to show Bragg Washington's letter.

"Thanks, Harry," Taylor said, and then hung up.

Out of the corner of his eye, Bell caught the newsflash on the TV screen about the *Mistral*. Before Bell could fully absorb it, the handset rang again. This time it was Lewis on the line. "Harry," Lewis said, "I'm here with Tracy. She's open to cooperate but wants to know what the plan is." "Fair enough," replied Bell. "Can you put her on speaker? Hi, Tracy, it's Harry Bell." Tracy knew instantly who he was but had no idea why he was involved in trying to help her. Bell, guessing that Tracy was more than a bit confused, added, "There are a few of us who are very interested in protecting the Constitution and ensuring a peaceful transition of power. Susan's part of the group. I'll explain more when we meet, but for now, we need to get you out of NYC and to somewhere you can be properly protected." Before anyone had a chance to react, Bell asked, "George, can you get Tracy and Elle onto the roof of the Met's main building at 6 p.m. sharp?" George replied, "Not easy, but I should be able to figure it out. I'm still a museum trustee." "Great," replied Bell. "General Charles Taylor can pick up then. Tracy is that okay?" Tracy's head was reeling at this point—the world's most powerful banker, the head of U.S. Northern Command, and her oldest friend from college. It didn't make a lot of sense, but it at least seemed genuine, and these were people with serious resources. "I guess," Tracy said finally. "It's not like I have a lot of options." "You don't," replied Bell, "unless you want to find out how Hawley plans to deal with you." "I would rather not," said Tracy. "Thanks—and we are on your side," replied Bell. "Susan, I'll be back in touch shortly with more details." Then he hung up.

As soon as Bell had ended one call, he dialed another. Taylor picked up just as the handset rang. "Yes, Harry." "I need you to do a pickup after West Point. Main roof of the Met Museum, NYC, at 6 p.m. sharp. It's Tracy and Elle Rockefeller. Destination is the Lodge." "Of course," Taylor stated—in the same tone he used to use when picking up the kids after school.

Bell's next call was to New Jersey—Julia Jackson. As soon as she picked up, Bell asked, "How's the Lodge?" Jackson replied, "It's stunningly beautiful here. I just wish we were here under different circumstances. How can I help?" "I need two things," Bell replied. "First, I need you to leak—through a different network, ideally Fox—that Hawley Oil's loans have been called and it's facing bankruptcy. Second, I need one reporter and one cameraman positioned at the top of the left-hand side of the steps in front of the Met Museum at 5:45 p.m. I'm going to arrange to have Tracy Rockefeller give them a short interview right before 6 p.m. Don't tell them who it is and make sure it's on tape and not live. Make sure they do not broadcast it before 6:30 p.m." "Got it and done," replied Jackson.

Bell then reconsidered, "On 2nd thought. Hold on the Hawley Oil leak for now. Let's use it when it's going to have the most impact."

Bell's next call was back to Lewis. "Susan, can you put me back on speaker?" With everyone now listening, Bell confirmed the plans for the pickup and asked Rockefeller if she'd mind speaking to the CBS crew right before being spirited away. Bell explained that after Hawley's *Mistral* announcement, showing the nation that she was alive and well was critical. Before Tracy could reply, Elle blurted out, "Mom, you have to do it. People need to be able to keep believing in you or they win." Tracy replied, "Agree. Make it happen."

Early Afternoon - Supreme Court

Lockwood slid a four-page draft to Hoyt. "Emergency administrative stay. Immediate effect. Enjoins any federal action that halts tallying of lawfully cast ballots."

Hoyt read, fixed a clause about equitable factors, and signed. "Circulate to the full Court. Release *per curiam* at 1:30 p.m." Hoyt looked up at the mural on the ceiling of Washington addressing the men at Valley Forge. "Now draft the curfew order," he told Lockwood. "Please get it released before the 3 p.m. conference—do it under your signature." Looking up one last time, Hoyt muttered under his breath, "Let's make the old man proud."

Mid Afternoon - Raven Rock

Clark strode into the fake Oval Office with a copy of the emergency administrative stay lifting the halt of the ballot tallying. Hawley was sitting behind the desk, with Harris sitting on the right-hand side couch, staring at the TV in the corner.

VOTE COUNTING MAY RESUME crawled across the bottom of one screen, and the country inhaled. Before Clark could open his mouth, Hawley muttered, "We know." Clark immediately replied, "We're already drafting a petition to have the stay lifted." "Good," Hawley said. "I expect they will also put a stay on the curfew—have the draft to get that lifted ready as well. I want you personally at the Supreme Court and in front of Hoyt by tomorrow morning. Might also be worth reminding Justices Coney and Bomgardner who put them on the Court."

Before Clark could take his leave, the door to the fake Oval opened again. An aide ushered Rockefeller's running mate, Chris Bolton, into the office. The aide then turned and silently exited.

"Chris, welcome," said Hawley as he got up to shake his hand. "You know Attorney General Clark and VP Harris." "I do, sir," replied Bolton. "What brings me here?" Hawley leaned back against the front edge of the fake **Resolute Desk** and said, "I'm sure you've heard the news about Rockefeller being lost at sea. The nation is fracturing. We need to pull it back together. With Rockefeller tragically gone, presenting a united political front will help calm the unrest. Therefore, I am offering you the vice-presidency. Harris will be resigning shortly, and I will have your appointment confirmed by Congress as soon as it reconvenes."

Harris sat on the couch, stunned and speechless. As Bolton's ambition was off the charts and his IQ sadly not, he immediately smiled and said, "I accept." "Great," said Hawley. "Go out and get prepped for the announcement. Let's tape it in fifteen and then release ahead of the evening news cycle—target 5 p.m. to make sure it's the lead story." Bolton turned as an aide opened the door and exited.

As soon as the door closed, Harris muttered, "Ted, what the fuck?"—using the President's first name for the first time in as long as anyone could remember. "Joe," Hawley replied, "unfortunately that aide you were with yesterday taped you. It would be horrible if that got out. Don't worry—your loyalty will be rewarded. You can have your choice of ambassadorships when this is all done." Hawley then opened a drawer on the desk and pulled out a letter of resignation for Harris to sign. He pushed it across toward Harris, got up, and prepared to exit the fake Oval Office. Right before going through the door, he turned to Harris and said, "Joe, would you mind signing that on your way out? I have to go prep for the announcement now."

As the door closed, the TV in the corner flashed with the announcement of Lockwood's emergency stay on the nationwide curfew. Harris was left alone, to sign and seethe.

Mid Afternoon - Supreme Court

The justices filed into their private conference room right at 3 p.m. on the dot. Despite the public perception that justices are either liberal or conservative, the truth was more nuanced. In

Hoyt's mind, his Court lined up with two liberals, two populists, and five moderates. For Hoyt, the key was holding the five moderates together.

Hoyt started, "As you all know, we have issued two emergency stays—on the vote count halt and the nationwide curfew. I expect the Justice Department will petition us later today to have those lifted immediately. When they do, the full Court will need to review and rule. We should expect to have this on the docket for tomorrow. I'll let you know if anything else comes up. Given what's happening outside, I've already arranged for extra security at the Court. Food and cots have been brought in for anyone who would like to stay. Let's meet back here at 10 a.m. tomorrow. Any questions?" No one spoke. They all just nodded and quietly left the room.

Late Afternoon – Outskirts - Washington, D.C.

The leader of the Mountain Men Militia pulled his top lieutenants into his trailer. "Boys, have you seen this?" he said, pointing at the TV. Across the screen ran the twin banners of the two Supreme Court emergency stays. "Boys," he said, "I don't think the Court understands the situation we're facing. Perhaps we should go down there tonight and provide them with a bit of guidance and encouragement." "That's the best idea I've heard all day," replied his No. 2. "I'll go muster the men. We can move in under the cloak of darkness. Won't they be surprised when they wake up in the morning."

Mid Afternoon - 993 Fifth Avenue - NYC

The group of six had now congregated in the living room. Post and Lewis sat on one couch, facing Tracy and Elle on the other. Vega and Whitman occupied the two armchairs at the ends.

"We need to figure out how we're going to pull this off without any of us getting picked up by Hawley's people," Tracy said. Post weighed in. "Tracy, you and Susan are the same age, similar build, similar hair color. If we put you in similar clothes—hair up, baseball hat pulled down, dark glasses—it'll be hard to tell you apart from twenty yards." Lewis leaned forward and added, "George is right. I can act as a decoy." Tracy then laid out the plan: "First, George, Elle, and Susan will go over to the Met around 5:30 p.m. George, take Susan and Elle up to Gallery 810, then use your trustee pass to access the emergency stairwell and unlock the door to the roof. The three of you will wait there, out of camera sight, until I arrive. At 5:50 p.m., I will leave the apartment with Vega and Whitman. I'll go straight up the steps, head down, and then walk to the far left behind the columns. Vega and Whitman will follow behind me, grab the camera crew on the steps, and lead them over to where I'm standing behind the last column. I'll then give a short interview before disappearing inside through the side door and hustling up to Gallery 810. In parallel, Vega and Whitman will keep the news crew from following me inside. They will then walk the news crew back to the bottom of the main steps. At a minute before 6 p.m., Elle and I will open the door and go out onto the roof, using a small flashlight to identify our location. Taylor should then be able to fly in, load us, and leave. Shortly after 6 p.m., Susan and George will walk out through the Met's main entrance, go down to Fifth Avenue, and hail a cab—waving to the news crew right before getting into the taxi. Vega and Whitman, you can come back up here and lay low until this is all blown over. Susan and George can then head to Penn Station and catch the Acela to D.C., after ditching the hat, glasses, and sweaters in the taxi."

5:00 p.m. - West Point

Bragg walked the terrace above the Hudson, hands bare to the cold. He had arrived early, flying into West Point's private airstrip from Raven Rock on the jet reserved solely for the Chairman's use.

Taylor flew himself in the Black Hawk. He had two trusted crew members on board with him and two Apaches as escorts. They landed on the old parade ground. As he disembarked, Taylor signaled to the crews to stay with the birds.

Taylor made his way over to the terrace. When he arrived, Bragg was there already, leaning on the rail. Taylor saluted the senior officer; in return, Bragg extended a hand. "No staff," Bragg said. "No recordings," Taylor returned.

They stood shoulder to shoulder, two old soldiers pretending to admire a river. "This is getting messy," Taylor said softly. "It's the last thing the country needs." "I know," Bragg said. "Hawley is obsessed with staying in power. The more he feels it slipping away from him, the more desperate the measures I'm afraid he will order." "If he orders something unlawful, unconstitutional… we swore an oath," Taylor replied.

As Taylor's last word came out of his mouth, he remembered Washington's decree, safely folded in his jacket's breast pocket. "And if you can't stop the order, don't transmit it (and log the refusal)," Taylor followed. Bragg laughed, sadly, like a man resigned to his fate. "Simple… but you don't know him like I do. If I don't transmit it (and log the refusal), he's likely to issue the order directly to you." "Let's try simple first," Taylor said. "If he approaches me directly, we can deal with it then."

At that moment, both of their Pentagon-issued cell phones pinged. It was the alert on Harris being replaced by Bolton. Taylor looked at Bragg and said, "James, he will fuck you over in the end as well." Bragg just nodded. Before turning to leave, Taylor added, "James, do you remember why Washington called West Point 'the key of America'?" "I do, Charles," Bragg replied, adding, "In many ways it still is."

The two generals then saluted, shook hands, and parted ways. As Bragg was walking away, he turned and said, "Just so you know, I'm headed to the Pentagon now. My plan is to stay there until this is over." Taylor nodded and smiled, thinking to himself that this was the first really smart move Bragg had made in the last couple of days.

5:20 p.m. - 993 Fifth Ave

"Mom," Elle shouted, "you need to see this. Hawley just announced that Harris is resigning as VP and being replaced by Chris Bolton." One word came out of Tracy's mouth: "Slimeball." Then, "This changes nothing. You, Susan, and George are leaving in ten minutes."

5:40 p.m. - Over the Hudson River

Arriving back at the parade ground, Taylor signaled the crews over to the door of the Black Hawk. Taylor's orders were simple: radio silence, full stealth mode. They were to fly down the Hudson River at a 300-foot ceiling, staying under the radar. Upon reaching Manhattan Island, Taylor was going into the city to make a pickup at 18:00 sharp. The two Apaches were to hold over the Hudson until he returned. They were then to follow him to an undisclosed location in the Ohio River Valley. The crews saluted, and the three helicopters took off in formation.

5:50 p.m. - Met Steps

Having made her way successfully across Fifth Avenue without being identified, Tracy waited for the **CBS crew** to be escorted to her. Vega and Whitman arrived with the **CBS crew** right on time, and Tracy did a quick intro. After the shock on the anchor's face settled, Tracy said, "Can we please roll?" With the camera light now red, Tracy said, "My fellow Americans, I want you to know that Elle and I are alive and well. I am aware of the moves the current administration has made, and I am patiently waiting for the courts to rule on the legality. While every American has a constitutional right to protest, I ask that we all do so peacefully. Thank you, and God bless."

And with that, she turned and disappeared through the side door into the museum and made her way up to Gallery 810.

To the security camera, it looked like Tracy Rockefeller walked into Gallery 810 at 5:58 p.m. and then exited back toward the main entrance at 6:01 p.m. Rockefeller was then seen walking out the main doors with an unidentified friend and getting into a taxi around 6:05 p.m. Shortly after, she was swallowed by New York City's unrelenting traffic.

In the interval, a low helicopter flew in near silently and picked two individuals off the roof of the Met.

Late Evening - Townhouse

The handset on the coffee table finally rang. Bell grabbed it immediately. Taylor's voice came on the line. "All set, Harry. Went smoothly. Rockefeller is at the Lodge. Will debrief on the discussion with Bragg tomorrow."

102

Bell was about to turn off the light when the handset rang again. "It's Susan," Lewis said. "I'm still in Manhattan, and I have Post with me." "What happened?" asked Bell. "New York traffic," replied Lewis. "We were planning on taking the 6:45 Acela to D.C., but traffic was so bad we didn't get to Penn Station until ten after seven. When we arrived, there were people streaming out of the station. I asked the taxi driver what was going on and he said it looks like they've canceled all departing trains. We guessed Hawley's people had seen Tracy's interview at 7 p.m. and immediately moved to close off Manhattan." "Where are you now?" asked Bell. "Crypt, Trinity Church. Same place Post brought Rockefeller a couple of days ago. We'll be fine; George knows places down here that history forgot generations ago." "It might be a few days before I can get you both out," Bell stated. Lewis replied, "Understood, but you owe me one very expensive dinner when this is done."

Day 4 – Chess Match

Early Morning – Secure Line (Townhouse ↔ The Lodge)

The Lodge was built in the middle of the 1.5-million-acre Martha Dandridge Conservation Land Trust. There was only one road in and one road out. No one was ever spotted entering or exiting. The last mile to the Lodge was via a tunnel running through the mountains, which all but assured that no one would ever stumble upon it. While most of the buildings were underground and built into the mountainside, those that were above ground were amply camouflaged by both terrain and tree cover from the eyes of any prying satellites. A limitless supply of hydropower kept the whole place running. Unlike the Townhouse, which only needed a bare minimum of staff, there were far more people employed at the Lodge, as it was the operational heart of the 13. All of them had résumés that included time in the Secret Service, CIA, FBI, or Special Forces. They all understood discretion to their cores. For most, after a lifetime of government service, they highly appreciated the high salaries, and excellent retirement benefits the Martha Dandridge Trust provided.

As the sun was starting to peek through the curtains, the secure handset on Tracy's nightstand buzzed once.

As soon as she picked up, "Governor Rockefeller," the voice said, "it's Harry Bell." "I'm sending a document to the iPad in your room," Bell said. A message alert flashed up and, when Tracy pressed it, a high-resolution scan of a single vellum page, browned at the edges, appeared. It had 22 signatures at the bottom, but the one that immediately caught her eye was George Washington's.

"Drawn up in the first year of his second term," Bell said, voice even. "Washington and Chief Justice Jay set this in motion when they'd seen enough of how democracies fail. They called it simply the Decree, and it carries more force than any amendment."

Tracy read the neat, angular script twice—the second time repeating out loud:

"The Guarantors act only when the Constitution is threatened, including if a President refuses to yield lawful succession or dissolves the People's representation."

"The Chief Justice holds the key and knows the Decree; he alone may invoke the Decree and charge the Guarantors to take action."

"Appointment is for life; succession is by sealed designation, held by the first among equals."

"Remove the threat, then return power to its lawful channels at the earliest hour."

And then Rockefeller went silent. Bell gave her a few minutes to absorb the magnitude of what she had just read before stating, simply, "Questions?"

Finally, Rockefeller replied, "Enough to fill a week. But in terms of what I need to know and understand now:"

— The Decree has been invoked by Chief Justice Hoyt.

— Harry, you are the first among equals.

— The actions you are taking are to ensure a lawful succession, and you believe Hawley is trying to prevent this.

— Once a lawful succession has happened, the Guarantors will disappear back into the background.

— You have the power and resources to make this all happen.

— Hawley is unaware of your existence.

To which Bell simply said, "Yes."

And then Rockefeller said quietly, "And you are helping me as you believe that, once all the votes are counted, I will be the next President."

To which Bell again replied, "Yes."

Rockefeller then asked, "In terms of the cleanup afterwards?"

Bell replied, "We haven't got there yet, but our role will be very limited. Our only interest will be those at the very top who directly took action that threatened the Constitution."

Rockefeller paused again before simply stating, "Do I want to know what will happen to them?"

Bell: "Better you don't. Our actions are not subject to any judicial or other review."

Tracy stared at the last line on the screen until the words blurred. Remove the threat, then return power to its lawful channels.

The iPad felt heavier than it should in her hands.

"So that's it?" she said. "You invoke this thing and suddenly you're above the law?"

"You can call it above, or just outside," Bell said. "And it's intended to be brief."

"That's supposed to be reassuring?" Tracy looked up. The room's imposing beams and floor to ceiling picture windows belonged in a luxury resort, not in a secret constitutional failsafe. "Harry, where I come from, people with private armies and secret decrees are called something else entirely."

"We don't have an army," Bell said. "We just have limited resources and our brains. It's not a particularly pleasant duty."

The secure line, buzzed once, Bell asked, Tracy, do you mind if I add Chief Justice Hoyt to the call? Before she could answer, Bell conferenced Hoyt in. Hoyt started, "Tracy, Washington did not give the 13 a license to rule. He gave them a fire extinguisher and made them promise to put it back when the fire's out."

Tracy, grasping, "But you're manipulating markets, the media, using governors...."

"We're actually just trying to make sure the rightful winner of the election ends up in the White House," Bell added with the calm that comes from many a corporate political battle. "I'm guessing that would be your desired outcome as well?"

"Yes," Tracy said. "But what I don't want is a coup facilitated by a piece of centuries old vellum."

"If this were a coup," Hoyt said, "We would have dissolved Congress and proclaimed you President last night."

"That's insane," Tracy said. "This is still the United States."

"Hawley's moving towards a declaration of martial law," Hoyt answered. "That's the environment we are now operating in."

Bell then added, "Tracy, the Decree says what we can do and what we must not. We can act only when the Constitution is under direct attack. We must act only to restore it, and then we fade back into the background, where we have been existing quietly for over two centuries now."

"Fade away," Tracy repeated. "While the rest of us clean up whatever mess you leave, and who holds you accountable if you get it wrong?" Tracy asked. "If you decide the 'threat' is just someone you don't like? Or the wrong party wins too many times in a row?"

"We swore an oath," Bell said. "We live by Washington's rules. We have the knowledge that if we overreach, we destroy the very thing we swore to guard."

"That's not accountability," Tracy said. "There are no checks and balances on you."

Silence hung over the line. Finally, Tracy intoned, "Harry, if I go along with this, if I accept your help, I'm tied to it," she said. "If I become President because a secret club found a fire extinguisher in a tomb at Mount Vernon, and they decided to use it, how am I different from Hawley?"

"Because he's trying to stay in power by ignoring the will of the people," Bell said softly. "And you're going to be given power because that's what the people have willed."

She opened her mouth, closed it. The distinction was real, even if not comfortable.

"My allegiance is to the Constitution," she said.

"So is ours," Bell said. "Same person who will deliver it to you, delivered it to us and he just happens to be on his call."

Tracy let out a long breath through her nose. "I need you to understand something," she said. "If I make it through this, if I end up in that office, I'm not going to be your puppet."

"Good," Bell said. "Puppets make terrible Presidents. And once we have made it through this, you are on your own because we will disappear again."

"Then let's remove the threat," Rockefeller said. "And I still need to get my head around this whole thing."

Rockefeller, after another long pause: "What do you need from me?"

Bell: "Help us keep the temperature down. The situation Hawley is creating is highly volatile, and we want to keep people from getting killed and the country splintering."

Rockefeller looked up from the iPad and asked, "Who's with me at the Lodge?"

Bell replied, "Six of us right now," he said. "Virginia, Georgia, New Jersey, Maryland, North Carolina, and South Carolina. Pennsylvania—General Taylor, who dropped you off—has gone back to Norfolk Naval Station. The two Apache helicopters that provided your escort are still on site and will remain there until this is over... just in case we get any trespassers. I'm in D.C. at the Townhouse, and just so you know, Post and Lewis are still in NYC but safe. Plan right now is to see how events unfold this morning and then make a call on our next moves."

"In response," Rockefeller said, "Harry—thank you for showing me."

Bell added, "By the way, if you still have your personal cell phones you can use them at the Lodge. Any attempt to trace will lead to a McDonald's in downtown Chicago."

As the line went dead, Elle entered Tracy's bedroom via a connecting door.

Elle asked, "Mom, do you know where we are?"

Tracy: "Somewhere in the Ohio River Valley. We are safe here, and these people are on our side."

Elle replied, "Who are they?"

Tracy responded, "That's a very long story for once this is all over. Please just trust me— and you can trust them."

9:00 a.m. - Chief Justice's Private Chambers - Supreme Court

The Court's marble halls ate egos. The weight of the place made proud men small. Attorney General Mark Clark's shoes scuffed along the carpet as he slowly walked toward the Chief Justice's private chambers. A Marshal opened the Chief Justice's door, waved Clark in, then shut it firmly behind him.

Hoyt, seated behind his imposing 18th-century desk, looked up and nodded toward a chair on the other side.

"Mr. Chief Justice," Clark began, tone smooth as any career politician, "the President wanted me to convey that continued judicial interference in executive-branch decisions in our hour of national peril is not appreciated. The President feels strongly that the Court is overstepping its constitutional boundaries. And to be clear, it will have consequences."

Hoyt studied him the way an apex predator examines potential prey. "Should I consider that a threat?"

"I'm simply reminding you of the separation of powers as set forth in the Constitution." Clark leaned in over the desk. "If you insist on continuing to blur the line, we will return the favor. Remember when Stalin asked Churchill, 'How many divisions does the Pope have?'"

Hoyt's voice never rose. "We follow the Constitution. That is the job." He picked up a card from his desk—one of those elegant, old-fashioned engraved ones—and wrote calmly:

A clear separation of powers is essential to prevent tyranny — A. Hamilton.

He handed it to Clark as if he were a student who had just received a failing grade.

Clark smiled thinly. "I will pass along your regards to the President."

"And you might remind him about how history remembers Stalin," Hoyt said, and rang for the Marshal.

10:00 a.m. - Conference Room - Supreme Court

The Justices filed in without clerks, phones, or notes. Coats over chairs. Coffee cooling.

Hoyt opened without pomp. "Two questions before us: Can the President halt state ballot tallies? Can he impose a nationwide curfew? We will address both. First: argument."

Bomgardner went first, chin high. "The President's Article II powers, coupled with emergency statutes, allow temporary measures to preserve civic order. Elections require order. We have chaos and unrest in several major cities—have you seen the militia gathered nearby?"

Lockwood's reply was surgical. "The Elections Clause assigns authority to the states. Counting lawfully cast ballots is the very definition of a republican government. Order adjunct to law? Yes. Order that displaces it? No."

Coney commented, "Chaos has consequences."

Justice Conner added: "And when the chaos is being generated and stoked by the Executive Branch?"

Lockwood stated, "We are dancing dangerously close to tyranny."

Hoyt didn't weigh in. He watched the room like a coach, knowing his star players would score when he needed them to. When he finally spoke, it was to procedure: "We vote."

Ballots slid. Six landed one way, three the other.

"Opinion assignments," Hoyt said.

Lockwood took the majority. "I'll make it short and sweet," he said. "The federal government has no role in state tallies. The curfew lacks lawful predicate."

Bomgardner claimed the dissent, anger in his eyes. "Emergency presidential power is constitutional and sweeping, even if unpopular. This is interference."

"Release at three p.m.," Hoyt concluded. "Per curiam for the orders; opinions to follow shortly. For our safety, I want us all in the building when they are released."

The Justices then filed back to their private chambers.

Once her door was closed, Coney pulled her cell phone out of her pocket and dialed Clark's private line. "Both rulings are not going your way; release is at 3 p.m."

Clark replied, "Understood, and will pass the message along. We appreciate the call and loyalty."

11:00 a.m. - Replica Oval - Raven Rock

The control-room screen displayed the current nationwide state of play.

Led by Texas Governor Ross Hogg, 18 governors across the South and Bible Belt had declared they would not restart counting and/or would maintain National Guard deployments at tally sites under their own "public safety" rationale. All were also enforcing the curfew.

Fifteen governors on the East and West Coasts had ignored the curfew, ordered that vote counting be resumed, and kept their National Guards in the barracks, with police handling civil disturbances. Virginia Governor Bill McLean had emerged as this bloc's spokesperson and given several TV interviews defending his position.

Seventeen governors had issued statements indicating they were fence-sitting and waiting to see which way the wind was blowing. Ohio was the first to state: "monitoring conditions," "coordinating with local officials," "urging calm." The rest followed shortly with similar sentiments.

Hawley took it all in from the open door leading to the fake Oval Office. A capillary in his temple pulsed. In Hawley's mind, the math was simple: win over the majority of the fence-sitters, and he could manipulate the process to deliver himself another four years in the White House.

The phone in Hawley's jacket rang once. He grabbed it quickly, spun, and closed the fake Oval's door behind him. "Yes," he answered, like a man in a hurry.

The voice on the other line said simply, "It's Clark. I delivered the message to Hoyt. He did not take it well. The Court is 6–3 against us. Rulings will be released at 3 p.m."

Hawley said, "Understood. Stay in D.C. but keep away from the Court. Any news on Mount Vernon LLC?"

Clark replied, "Nothing."

Hawley commanded, "Call that asshole at Treasury—Cohen. Tell him he has 48 hours to make it go away, or he will be looking for a new job."

Clark replied, "Understood."

Hawley dropped the cell phone back into his pocket and strode across the Oval to a private conference room on the other side. Harris, Bolton, and McCollins were all sitting around the table, staring at a bank of monitors. Front and center was the "state of play" across the states, with talking heads and local news shots filling the rest of the screens.

Hawley entered the room. "Where's Bragg?"

Harris replied, "Pentagon—went there after his meeting with Taylor."

Hawley commented, "Fine. Probably better that Boy Scout isn't hearing this anyway. Harris, your people in D.C.—get them to disrupt the Court. Tell them whatever you need to. This needs to happen before 3 p.m."

Harris, pale and quiet since yesterday's humiliation, simply nodded yes.

Hawley then ordered, "Bolton, get on the phone with the fence-sitters. I need those governors on our side. Remind them who is President. Give me a reason to keep you around—especially as it turns out Rockefeller didn't drown off the Jersey shore."

Hawley added, "Conference Clark in. I need him to hear this. McCollins, I need you back in D.C. Call the House into order tonight. I'm invoking the Insurrection Act and federalizing the Guard. I need the House to back me up. Call Webster and make sure the Senate does the same."

Hawley then ordered, "Clark, call Bragg and inform him that I am invoking the Insurrection Act and federalizing the Guard. He is to stand by for orders. Release this to the press at noon."

12:00 p.m. - The Townhouse - Washington, D.C.

Bell sat in a small office off the main conference room monitoring the news feeds. He had a wall of screens plastered on the wall across from the desk. On the feeds Bell had been watching:

Tulsa — National Guard posted by the governor met a county police line who'd just been told to stand down by a judge enforcing the Court's orders. A pushed shield, a reflexive baton, and then a shot from somewhere no camera caught. Two down, dozens trampled.

Louisville — Militia trucks boxed a bridge; city police flanked, then flashed badges and let marchers through. Cheers in one lane, curses in the other.

Phoenix — Clerks rolled new bins to counting tables as observers argued about inches and sightlines; a retired judge with a bullhorn made both sides laugh and then shut up.

Dallas — A tired Guardsman took off his helmet and said to a deputy: "I'm from Plano. I'm not your enemy." The deputy nodded. "Then help me keep them from killing each other."

The secure handset rang; it was Hoyt.

Hoyt said, "Afternoon, Harry. I'm here with Walter, and I'm putting you on speaker."

Bell replied, "I had a long conversation with Rockefeller this morning. She's OK and understands our role. She will help when we need it. I've got Burr here as well. You'll are on speaker."

Hoyt: "Her brief interview on CBS last night worked well. Hawley is really overplaying his hand now. I had a short visit from the Attorney General this morning. He made it known that if the Court didn't back off there would be consequences. I have it all on tape in case we ever need it."

Bell: "He is Hawley's bagman."

Hoyt: "On the two issues before the Court, vote was 6–3. We are drafting now and aim to release at 3 p.m. Also, separate from recent events, I've known there was a leak on the Court, so I have had Coney's phone tapped. She called Clark right after the vote to let him know the rulings."

Bell: "I'm looking at the newsfeed across the desk—looks like Hawley's already reacted. Headline: 'President has invoked the Insurrection Act and is federalizing the National Guard.'"

Hoyt: "It was only a matter of time."

Burr: "When do we remind him of:

18 U.S.C. § 592 (prohibition of troops at polls), which prohibits stationing 'troops or armed men' by military or federal officials at the polls in a general or special election except when necessary 'to repel armed enemies of the United States';

18 U.S.C. § 593 (military election interference), which prohibits members of the military from interfering 'in any manner with an election officer's discharge of his duties';

and

18 U.S.C. § 595 (governmental election interference), which prohibits government employees from using official authority in connection with federally financed activity to interfere with or affect a federal election; and that under the 'bad faith' test we can stay the order?"

Bell: "Nate, on the first two, we aren't going to—Taylor will—and it's a discussion I believe he will have to have with Bragg. We will then let Bragg deliver the news to Hawley. Suggest we hold off with any judicial 'stay' on the order for now. Hawley has just massively overreached, and the nation—along with a few governors—are about to find out he doesn't have the military behind him."

12:10 p.m. - Supreme Court - Washington, D.C.

Once the call was finished, Hoyt summoned the Court's Sergeant at Arms.

Hoyt: "John, I would like you to quietly call off the U.S. Marshals who are guarding the building. They should disperse, as I don't want anyone to get hurt. If the militia that camped nearby starts to move toward the Court, hit the alarm button and it will seal the building. I had a few extra security features installed as part of the 2025 renovation. We did learn something from January 6th. I'm not having some uninvited guest putting his feet up on my desk. Sadly, we aren't necessarily always who we think we are. The Court will be fine."

John, the Sergeant at Arms: "Yes, sir. Immediately."

12:10 p.m. - Townhouse - Washington, D.C.

As soon as the call with Hoyt was over, Bell placed a secure call to General Charles Taylor at Norfolk Naval Station. Taylor was alone in the Base Commander's Office.

Bell: "Afternoon, Charles. Have you seen Hawley's latest move?"

Taylor: "I have. How do you suggest we handle it?"

Bell: "I want to play this out. He is forcing everyone to put their cards on the table and pick a side. It will make the cleanup easier, though."

Taylor: "He will go through Bragg. When Bragg calls, I will stall and insist on a legal review based on §§ 592 and 593 before implementing any orders."

Bell: "Technically the D.C. Guard reports to you now?"

Taylor: "It does, as Hawley's federalized it. All troops on U.S. soil technically now do."

Bell: "Great. See if you can string out any definitive response until tomorrow. My guess is that when Hawley is told he can't have the National Guard storm voting stations, he will try to first fire Bragg and then you. We will get a Supreme Court ruling that Hawley can't remove you for refusing to follow an illegal order. By the time Hawley gets around to challenging that, he will be facing impeachment charges under § 595 (governmental election interference), which will make the whole thing moot."

Taylor: "McCollins will never allow a vote on impeachment."

Bell: "McCollins will not be Speaker by tomorrow morning. Maryland—Fitzwilliams—will be. He's on his way here from the Lodge as we speak."

Taylor: "Jesus, Harry, did you tutor Machiavelli in a prior life?"

Bell laughed and said goodbye before immediately dialing New Jersey—Julia Jackson—who was at the Lodge.

Bell: "Julia, afternoon—if you haven't seen her, Rockefeller and her daughter are at the Lodge. I'm going to conference her in."

Bell: "Tracy, good afternoon. I also have Julia Jackson on the line. Julia, can you use the studio at the Lodge and do a 15–20 minute interview with Tracy? Suggest you shoot it with a green screen and then make it appear that you are both in Manhattan. This will throw Hawley's dogs off. Tracy, if you are comfortable doing this, I would like to get a bit more aggressive and increase the pressure on Hawley. Key messages:

• Based on independent exit polls, you believe you have won the presidential election by a wide margin.

• The vote tally needs to be completed peacefully and quickly. While every American has the right to protest, it must be done peacefully.

• You have seen no evidence of voter fraud or foreign interference in the election as Hawley has claimed. Challenge him to produce the evidence.

• Remind the military that their duty is to follow only those orders that are lawful.

• Your safety has been threatened, which is why you have kept a low profile.

• Chris Bolton will not be your Vice President."

Rockefeller: "Agreed. Then what comes next?"

Bell: "Another public appearance, probably tomorrow. Let's discuss where later."

Jackson: "Suggest we run this as a Special Report right after the 6 p.m. news."

Bell: "Perfect."

12:15 p.m. - Private Quarters – Raven Rock

Harris picked up his cell and dialed. The phone at the other end rang twice before the leader of the Mountain Men, Cletus Smith, picked up.

Harris: "I've seen that your men are all in position in front of the Supreme Court."

Smith: "We are, boss. Just say the word."

Harris: "Well, you might want to go inside soon and help the good Justices with their decision making."

Smith: "We would be glad to."

1:00 p.m. - Supreme Court -Washington, D.C.

The Mountain Men began to leave Senate Park and walk toward the Supreme Court. It was an unruly gaggle of men in surplus store camouflage, plastic helmets, plate carriers, hand-held radios, waving flags from prior failed rebellions. Several had AR-15s slung over their shoulders, along with gas masks, baseball bats, pistols shoved into waistbands, and backpacks carrying Molotov cocktails.

As they turned the corner onto First Street, word went out on the radios that the Court building was undefended. One joked that the U.S. Marshals must be on a lunch break. With that, the crowd surged forward. As they did, there was a loud bang as massive metal shutters came down over all the windows and the blast-proof doors sealed shut.

Undeterred, the Mountain Men stormed up the stairs, metal bars and baseball bats pounding against the main doors. Several pulled Molotov cocktails out and hurled them against the building, splattering glass and burning fuel on their compatriots who had been pushed up against the building by the crowd surging behind them.

Inside, the Justices all watched the chaos unfold on the monitors in their main conference room, with John, the Sergeant at Arms, and his two key lieutenants standing next to him right behind the Chief Justice's seat.

John: "The building is secure. They have no way in. We have several weeks of provisions stored on site along with our own secure communications and power supply. The Court can continue to function."

Hoyt: "Make no mistake, Hawley is behind this. Clark came by this morning and basically threatened me with this."

Coney, looking very shaken said, "Shall we try to negotiate with them—get them to withdraw?"

Lockwood: "I think at this point we just alert emergency personnel that they will have a number of burn victims incoming. Once they realize they can't get into the building, they will disperse. If not, then we can have it mopped up once they burn off a bit more energy."

Hoyt: "John, would you mind playing the recording of Coney's call to Clark this morning?"

Coney: "Stop. I've done nothing illegal."

Hoyt: "That's up to a court to decide. Or you can resign once this is all over and your indiscretions stay in this room."

Coney: "You're an ass, Anthony."

Hoyt: "John, please take Justice Coney and lock her in the basement holding room. Make sure you pat her down and remove any communication devices she still has on her."

Lockwood: "I've got to get back to my desk and finish the majority opinions."

Hoyt: "Thanks. Given what's going on outside, I would like to move up the timetable and issue the orders at 2 p.m."

As they were filing out of the conference room, Bomgardner texted Clark, "Hoyt has just taken Coney out."

The text arrived on three screens simultaneously—Clark's, Hoyt's, and one in Bell's office at the Townhouse.

Upon seeing it, Hoyt immediately called Bell on the secure handset.

Hoyt: "Assume you just saw the other mole's text."

Bell: "I did. Suggest you leave him in place and make him feel secure. We might be able to use him later."

Hoyt: "Agree, and I will let Lockwood know."

2:00 p.m. - Hawley's Private Quarters - Raven Rock,

Hawley sat on the couch staring at the split screen on the wall in front of him. On one side there was a massive headline reading "Supreme Court Under Siege"; on the other, "The President has invoked the Insurrection Act and is federalizing the National Guard."

On the other side of the room, Bolton and Harris sat quietly.

Hawley smiled at the scenes of Molotov cocktails exploding against the Supreme Court building. He muttered out loud to no one in particular, "I hope Hoyt has finally gotten the message."

Before the last word left his lips, a new banner appeared at the bottom of the screen: "Supreme Court issues permanent stays on the executive orders stopping the tallying of votes and the nationwide curfew." Ruling is 6–3 with opinions to follow.

Hawley: "Bold of him to still go ahead given the angry mob at his doorstep. I hope he doesn't have dinner plans."

Hawley's cell rang. Clark came up on the screen.

Hawley: "Let me put you on speaker. I've got Bolton and Harris here."

Clark: "I just heard from Bomgardner—Hoyt's taken Coney out."

Hawley: "Does Hoyt suspect Bomgardner as well?"

Clark: "I don't think so, or he would have been taken out as well."

Hawley: "Good. Suggest you come back to Raven Rock; it could get really ugly in D.C. shortly. Any news on Rockefeller?"

Clark: "None. She's gone to ground. Bolton—has she reached out?"

Bolton: "It's been dead silence—nothing, not even a message to confirm she is alive."

Hawley: "Let's let this news cycle burn itself out. I will order the Guard to move in the morning. Bolton and Harris, what's the latest count on the governors?"

Harris: "I have a few more leaning our way. They have promised statements in time for the evening news cycle."

2:30 p.m. - Guard Unit – Austin, Texas

"Bravo Company, this is Battalion command. Move to staging area Baker Two. Mission is to secure ballot storage facility at the county center. Repeat, secure ballot storage facility. Rules of engagement: standard civil support."

Sergeant Lena Ortiz sat in the driver's seat of the Humvee and listened without touching the ignition.

Private First Class Kline, looked over from the passenger seat. "Ma'am?"

"Where's the threat?" she asked quietly.

"Ma'am?"

"That's what the order doesn't say," Ortiz went on. "Is someone trying to burn the building down? Steal the ballots? Because if not, we're not securing a facility. We're interfering in an election."

Kline swallowed. He was twenty, and now very nervous "Battalion says"

"I know what Battalion says," Ortiz said. The radio crackled again, impatient. "Bravo Actual, confirm movement."

The convoy engines around them rumbled to life one by one.

Ortiz picked up the handset. Her thumb finally touching the transmit button, keeping her voice calm. "We copy movement to Baker Two. Be advised: will proceed at reduced speed. Request written ROE clarification from JAG on site before entry."

A beat of silence. Then, "Copy, Bravo. Proceed. JAG review pending."

Kline let out a breath he hadn't realized he was holding. "We're still going?"

"We're always going," Ortiz said. "Question is how fast and with what we're willing to do when we get there."

She turned the key. The Humvee coughed and caught. In her side mirror she saw a line of familiar young faces under helmets, nervous.

She eased the truck into gear and rolled out, slow enough that anyone watching could see they weren't in a hurry to become someone's pawn.

3:00 p.m. - Governor's Mansion - Montgomery, Alabama,

Governor Kay Wallace was sitting in her office with her three key aides watching the news feeds. The siege of the Supreme Court was dominating the headlines, and crews were now on site live-streaming both pictures and interviews with leaders of the militia. Cletus Smith's face appeared on the screen. The title below identified him as the Mountain Men's commander. Before he even got asked a question, Smith went on a diatribe, spouting that they were there defending freedom; that the Supreme Court was filled with pedophiles and communists; that they only took orders from the President; that the deep state was trying to put their pawn, Tracy Rockefeller, into the White House; and that he was in direct communication with VP Harris.

Wallace turned to her aides and said, "That very last part I believe. This is getting way out of hand. Hawley's lost the plot. Attacking the Supreme Court is about the most un-American thing I can imagine. They might as well have spit on Bear Bryant's grave. I'm ordering the Alabama Guard back to their barracks, vote tallying is to resume immediately, and we are lifting the curfew. Send out the orders immediately."

Her chief aide asked, "But ma'am, hasn't Hawley federalized the Guard?"

Wallace replied, "He has, but he hasn't issued any orders, so as far as I am concerned, they still report to me. If General Davidson questions the order, remind him that Hawley will likely no longer be President in a couple of weeks, but I will still be the Governor for at least the next several years."

Chief aide: "Clear, ma'am."

The first brick in Hawley's wall had just crumbled.

4:00 p.m. - Majority Leader's Office - The Senate,

John Webster leaned over his desk and buzzed his assistant, requesting another cup of coffee. His navy suit looked like he had slept in it. He had just had a very surreal discussion in his office with the Speaker of the House, Michael McCollins. McCollins had tried to convince him that they needed to pass a resolution backing up Hawley's actions, nullifying the election, and scheduling a new one in three months' time. McCollins indicated he was planning on calling the House into session at 6 p.m. to do so. What really shocked Webster, though, was how manic McCollins came across. He had transformed from alpha male to an overly excited eunuch. Webster stared out the window for a few minutes before picking up the handset Bell had given him and pressing dial.

Webster: "I just finished with Speaker McCollins. He's calling the House into session at 6 p.m. and is planning on passing a slew of resolutions backing up all of Hawley's moves."

Bell: "Perfect. Suggest you issue an order calling the Senate into session at 7 p.m. You can cancel it as soon as the House meets at 6 p.m. and send everyone home for the night. Call them back into session at 10 a.m. tomorrow. We will need the Senate's support then. Why don't you plan on coming back to the Townhouse afterward? I will arrange dinner and can update you on a few other things going on."

Webster: "You move in mysterious ways. Consider it all done."

4:15 p.m. – Townhouse - Washington, D.C.

Fitzwilliams sat across from Bell in a small office off the conference room. He had arrived earlier that afternoon from the Lodge. While Bell hadn't mentioned his presence to Webster, he had heard the whole conversation.

Bell: "How would you like to be the next Speaker of the House?"

Fitzwilliams laughed. "Not sure I have the votes. There are certain parts of the country where I am a lot less popular. I still can't get a decent table at a restaurant in Boston."

Bell: "Here's the plan: As soon as McCollins calls the House to order, propose a motion to vacate the chair. You will have more than enough support. This will catch McCollins completely off guard. He will likely get one of his cronies to try to table it. It will fail. Then move to have the resolution considered first thing tomorrow."

Fitzwilliams: "We have the votes for this?"

Bell: "I am sure we have what we need for tonight, and there will be more that swing our way by tomorrow morning."

Fitzwilliams: "I better head over to the Capitol. I will be back when we are done."

As soon as Fitzwilliams had left, Bell called Taylor.

Taylor: "Are Hoyt and Lockwood OK?"

Bell: "They're fine. Hoyt prepared for just this type of scenario years ago."

Taylor: "The fact that he even had to really chills me to the bone."

Bell: "Maybe once the dust settles—and if we show both compassion and wisdom—the nation will heal. Just perhaps we can make the Founders proud."

Taylor: "I hope so."

Bell: "Any word from Hawley or Bragg?"

Taylor: "Not yet."

Bell: "As the D.C. Guard now falls under your command, can you order them into the city and have them surround the Supreme Court?"

Taylor: "I can."

Bell: "Great. Do it as soon as the sun goes down. Ideally, we avoid any bloodshed. Also have them protect the Capitol Building and White House."

Taylor: "I know the D.C. Commander well. He's a good man with a calm, level head. If Bragg or Hawley call, I will tell them it's precautionary to protect key government installations."

Bell: "Thanks."

4:30 p.m. - Base Commander's Office - Norfolk Naval Station,

Taylor swung his chair around and exited the secure communication room. He turned to his chief of staff. "John, please get me General Tim McCarthy—D.C. National Guard—on the line. I will take it in my office."

The phone on the desk rang as Taylor was dropping back into his desk chair. He grabbed the receiver.

McCarthy: "Sir, what can I do for you?"

Taylor: "General McCarthy, I need you to deploy your men into Washington, D.C. They are to secure a perimeter around the Supreme Court, the Capitol Building, and the White House. Any and all protesters are to be kept well outside that perimeter. In regard to the group currently at the Supreme Court, those who want to leave peacefully should be allowed to do so but must surrender all offensive and defensive weapons. They are to be photographed and must show an ID, which should be scanned. Those who refuse have the choice of either being arrested or retreating back to the Court building. Ideally, we avoid any bloodshed, but if your men are fired upon, they have the right to defend themselves."

McCarthy: "Give me an hour and I will have my men in place."

Taylor: "Thanks, Tim. Call if you need any guidance or additional support. It's going to be a long night."

5:00 p.m. - Rockefeller's Suite - The Lodge,

Elle finally got around to pulling her cell phone out of the Faraday bag and turning it back on. As soon as the cell signal locked in, a text arrived. It was from her ex-boyfriend, Jimmy e. Elle clicked it to open: *Elle, hope you and your mother are safe. I'm at Raven Rock with the President. Things here are getting very weird. — Jimmy*

Elle copied it and forwarded it immediately to her mother.

6:30 p.m. - Sitting Room, Hawley's Private Quarters - Raven Rock,

Bolton, Harris, and Clark were spread out on the two couches facing each other, watching the bank of monitors on the far wall carrying the evening news programs. Hawley sat in an armchair at the top, feet up on the glass coffee table. Pictures of the siege at the Supreme Court and news that the D.C. Guard had moved into the city made for a good start to the segments in Hawley's mind. He muttered in Clark's general direction, "At least Bragg is doing what I need him to."

The later reports—that the Alabama Governor had ordered that state's Guard back to barracks, and that Georgia and both Carolinas had followed her lead—infuriated him. As he was turning to Harris to ream him, for failing to deliver expanded support, Tracy Rockefeller's picture appeared on the CBS feed with a red banner screaming **Special Report** underneath.

Hawley immediately stopped. "Turn up the volume."

Julia Jackson's face appeared on the screen, the New York City skyline in the background. Jackson started, "I'm here with presidential candidate Tracy Rockefeller."

The interview lasted 15 minutes, covering a range of topics, but all Hawley heard Rockefeller say was:

- She believes she has won the presidential election by a wide margin.
- The claims of voter fraud are nonsense, and Rockefeller challenged him directly to produce the evidence.
- She questioned why he hadn't condemned the violence at the Supreme Court—in particular her comment "that is not who we are as a nation" particularly stung.
- She promised to both govern from the middle and to put an end to the extreme populism and self-enrichment schemes of his administration.

Hawley found the interview grating; it barely registered that she announced Chris Bolton would not be her VP.

As the interview ended, Hawley turned to the group and said angrily, "She's still in New York City. Find her and shut her up."

At that moment, the feed from Fox flashed up with an alert: *House Speaker McCollins to face a 'motion to vacate the chair' vote. His speakership is now in jeopardy. McCollins has been a close ally of President Hawley and supporter of his claims of election fraud...*

Hawley threw the TV remote against the wall, his face now bright red. He then turned to Harris, nearly shouting, "I'm tearing up the resignation. Get those other militias moving—I want chaos in Chicago and Los Angeles by tomorrow morning before I deploy the Guard. Then call those governors back and let them know they need to do the right thing now. I'm out of patience."

Hawley then turned to Bolton and calmly said, "Your little Judas act has run its course. You should head home now."

Hawley stood up and walked to the door, turned, and signaled the others that they should follow. They followed him down the corridor and back into the main command center. There Hawley walked over to Special Agent North, leaned in, and said, "Bolton needs to disappear," before straightening up and saying more loudly, "North, please take Mr. Bolton to the airfield and put him on one of the G5s." He then turned to Bolton: "Just tell the pilots where you want to go."

Hawley turned and walked back to his quarters, head down. For the first time, it felt like he was no longer in complete control.

9:00 p.m. – Townhouse - Washington, D.C.

The mood in the lounge—where Bell, Fitzwilliams, Webster, and Lockwood had gathered—was almost jovial. The day had gone well, and the pieces were beginning to fall into place. Tomorrow, however, would be critical. If today was about field maneuvers with a few skirmishes, tomorrow the battle would commence. Bell signaled that it was time to get down to business.

Bell: "Walter, I'm sure the Court will receive a challenge to Hawley's Insurrection Act declaration by tomorrow morning, as there are several already moving up through the appellate courts. Suggest Hoyt schedules an early conference to review. Make sure the vote comes out in favor of Hawley. Bomgardner will leak it to Hawley, and he will then overreach, thinking the Court is suddenly swinging behind him. Schedule the ruling to be released at 3 p.m. but bury it.

By the time Bomgardner and Hawley figure out they have been had, it will be too late. Let Hoyt know he should be able to move on Bomgardner around midday."

Lockwood: "It will be a pleasure. I'm sure Coney will appreciate having Bomgardner's companionship. Just so you know, they do hate each other despite the shared allegiance to Hawley."

Bell: "Sam, that was masterful, and McCollins looked honestly shocked. How close do you think you are to having the votes needed for the Speaker's gavel?"

Fitzwilliams: "Harry, probably anywhere from 30–50 short, but I could have them in hand. It's hard to tell, as so many of the Representatives swing toward whichever way the wind is blowing."

Bell: "Sam, can you give me a list of names? I will have a $1 million donation made into each of their re-election accounts tonight from a Mr. George Washington with 'Honor, Duty, Sacrifice' written in the memo box. That should focus a few of your friends."

Fitzwilliams: "How are you going to pull that off?"

Bell: "Everyone forgets that the first U.S. capital was New York City. Washington spent the first two years of his presidency there and had an account at the Bank of New York. The bank never closed the account out of respect for their most famous customer. The money will be routed through that account."

Bell continued: "John and Sam, depending on how things go tomorrow morning, we might move on impeachment proceedings against Hawley and Harris in the afternoon. Let's check in around noon to see where we are."

Bell then pulled out the handset and said, "Let me conference Delaware—Kathy Curtis—and Tracy Rockefeller in."

Both picked up immediately.

Bell started: "Tracy, I thought the interview with Julia landed well. I don't know if you have met Kathy Curtis, the Governor of Illinois; she is one of us."

Curtis: "Harry, Tracy and I met back when she was Governor of New York. She is one of the people who inspired me to run for the governorship."

Rockefeller: "Kathy, good to reconnect. Harry, just want to let you know that Elle got a text from her ex-boyfriend. He's a Secret Service agent on Hawley's detail. He indicated Hawley and Co. are holed up at Raven Rock."

Bell: "That's really helpful. Let me get back to you on that."

Bell: "Tracy, I would like you to go to Chicago tomorrow morning and do a TV interview around 9:30 a.m. Julia will arrange it through a friend at ABC. As soon as the interview is done, we will have a crowd for you to address in front of the Wrigley Building. We should be able to helicopter you in and back out via the plaza across the street."

Bell: "Kathy, can you arrange security? We have word that one of Harris's militias may try to move downtown early tomorrow. We just need them kept well away from where Tracy is."

Curtis: "It will be tight, but I think we can pull it off. I will also have a wall of bullet-proof glass erected around the podium. The less time she is out in the open, the better."

After a pause, Curtis continued: "Chicago is called the Windy City for a reason—what's the backup if the helicopter can't fly?"

Bell: "Suggest you have a motorboat idling on the river below the plaza. The boat can then get her down the lake to a spot where she can pick up a backup helicopter. We are also going to have a couple of Apaches in the area to make sure no one interferes."

Rockefeller: "Kathy, I will see you tomorrow. Harry, can we talk in the morning to go through key communication points?"

Bell: "Of course. Suggest everyone get a good night's sleep. Tomorrow is going to be a long day."

9:30 p.m. - Tunnel Exit - Raven Rock

North and Bolton took the elevator up out of the bunker and to the surface. A black Ford Suburban was parked by the door, keys in the ignition. North climbed into the driver's seat with Bolton sitting right behind him. Not a word was said. North started the car and headed down the exit road. At the T-junction, North turned left. As soon as he had completed the turn, Bolton tapped him on the shoulder and said, "I thought the airfield I was flown into was to the right."

North nodded and replied, "You're right. Sorry—let me make a U-turn." The SUV then slowed and pulled to the right to create space for the turn. As North turned the wheel to the left, he swung his pistol up next to the headrest and pointed it directly back. As Bolton looked up, a single silenced shot brought darkness. North then turned the wheel back to the right and disappeared into the night.

Day 5 – History Smiles

7:00 a.m. - Replica Oval / Live on FOX & Friends - Raven Rock

The red light blinked. A producer gave the three hosts the windup signal. A phone icon pulsed on the bottom left of the screen.

"Mr. President, are you with us?"

Hawley didn't wait for the second prompt. "Hi. It's your favorite president." Friendly and warm did not come naturally. "Look, I'm sure the Supreme Court will uphold my Insurrection Act declaration. We *will* get the Guard out in the streets this afternoon and get order restored. The so-called 'loss' at the Court yesterday on vote tallying? Not really a loss, folks. The Court said it's a states' rights issue—so we'll work through the governors to get it done. And you know the majority of the governors are lining up with me on this."

One host: "There's a motion to vacate the Speaker's chair today—"

"Stupid move," Hawley cut in, chuckling. "A nothing congressman who got hit one too many times in the head playing football. The motion will fail. McCollins has my full support."

"And voter fraud?"

"It's really bad. And foreign interference—worse than anyone knows. I now have information that the deep state, funded in part by the *Rockefeller* family—yes, the Rockefellers—is involved. They're trying to steal an election to put one of their own in power. Tracy Rockefeller knows that. That's why she's gone into hiding."

Hawley then paused to let the "three fish" on the set firmly attach themselves to the hook he had just tossed. The FOX hosts dutifully gasped. Hawley's latest bombshell claims started scrolling across the bottom of the screen.

FOX Host 1: "Mr. President, do you have proof of this?"

Hawley: "I do and hope to be able to show it to the American people in a few days. First thing we need to do though is secure all the voting machines so we can do a proper forensic investigation."

FOX Host 2: "Mr. President, we look forward to seeing that. You know we have to be careful as the network did have to write a big check in the past on a similar claim."

Hawley: "Oh, this is much worse than that ever was. Tracy Rockefeller, and a few other members of her family, are likely looking at long jail sentences."

7:30 a.m. - The Townhouse - Washington, D.C.

Bell watched Hawley's FOX segment for a second time. When it was done, he clicked the monitor to mute. Bell then picked up a cream envelope and held it to the light. The vellum had browned at the edges, but the ink and handwriting were still clear.

"Sam," Bell said. "A letter from George for you to read on the House floor when the time comes."

Fitzwilliams: "But this wasn't part of the packet you and Hoyt recovered the other night."

Bell: "No, Washington wrote this one later, had it delivered to the first, first among equals and it's been passed down the line ever since. In many ways, it's his final warning and call for vigilance."

Bell then handed the letter to Fitzwilliams and said, "Please read it." Fitzwilliams started,

"Be wary of leaders who have become blinded by power and have forgotten that they are elected to serve the people.

Our Nation is forever fragile, dependent on the honor and sacrifices of men to survive. As the dusk falls on my Presidency and my days grow short, I would like to remind our young republic: be suspicious of those who seek power and majesty. A burning need for power is the worst affliction a man can have, it will create an ego that is insatiable. Believe in those that seek service and the honor that comes with it.

As I gaze today over both houses of Congress, I hope you will remember the sacrifices that allowed us to throw off tyranny. We have created a nation where all men are equal and possess inherent, unalienable rights to "Life, Liberty and the Pursuit of Happiness." These cannot be compromised or our whole great experiment will fail. The most powerful move a leader can ever make is to surrender power."

When he was finished, Fitzwilliams didn't say another word. He didn't need to. It was as if Washington had written the letter about Hawley.

Finally, he turned to Bell and said, "It's perfect."

8:00 a.m. - Conference Room - Supreme Court

Hoyt placed a stack of papers on the walnut conference table in front of him. "Emergency application to enjoin the President's proclamation under the Insurrection Act," he said. "We apply the usual test: likelihood of success, irreparable harm, and the public interest. Suggest we discuss for 30 and then vote."

Bomgardner, knowing that most of his peers' eyes were already upon him, started, "the statutes—10 U.S.C. §§ 251–254—exist for moments like this. Courts are not here to micromanage force posture. We step in only when the orders issued are clearly unlawful. This is currently well within the Executive's powers."

Lockwood leaned forward, elbows on the table. "At this point, it's a declaration, nothing more. No action has been taken that merits our involvement. At this point, it is unclear if the Executive has violated the "permitted range of honest judgment" test as set forth in Sterling v. Constantin. I believe it is also prudent for us to wait to see if the Executive has Congressional support for this move, as we will likely find that out later today.

Justice Conner shook her head. "With respect, this is little more than a move to intimidate and consolidate power. Governors are feeling threatened. Clerks at voting sites fear arrest. The sword doesn't have to be swung to be effective. Sometimes just showing it works.

Justice Jackson spoke softly. "We can acknowledge that threat and our concerns as to where this might lead while still not interfering with the Executive's power. A paragraph noting that this cannot be used to trample states' rights should suffice for now.

Lockwood nodded. "I concur, we rule not just on today's Executive but also for the future. A castrated Executive branch is not what the Constitution or Founders intended."

Bomgardner smiled. "I concur in the historic deference to the elected branches in exigency."

Conner looked to Hoyt. "Anthony, we're rewarding brinkmanship. He'll read it as permission to do as he pleases. We are enabling a potential dictator."

Hoyt spoke quietly but with conviction, "We need to respect precedent. The intention is not to expand executive authority. I do not believe we are being deferent nor abdicating our judicial independence. If the subsequent orders that the Executive issues cross the line, then we will deal with that when it lands in our docket. I suggest we now end the discussion and vote."

Eight folded slips of paper were passed to Hoyt. He opened each and quietly tallied them in his head. Six for denial without prejudice; two to grant the stay.

Hoyt raised his head and announced the outcome, adding, we will report this as 6-2 with Coney abstaining.

Hoyt summarized. "Per curiam: Application denied at this time. Public release at three this afternoon please."

Lockwood added. "I'll add a short concurrence pointing to Youngstown and the Elections Clause."

Bomgardner, relieved: "I'll note statutory history and the Executive's duty to keep order."

Conner, not quite believing or understanding what just went down stated, "I'll draft the dissent, then sarcastically added, "Well at least the crowd outside will like our ruling."

Lockwood caught Hoyt's eye as he was leaving, a single, slight nod was exchanged.

As soon as he was back in his chambers, Bomgardner picked up his cell phone and made the call to Clark that would seal his fate. As soon as Clark received the news, he passed it on to Hawley with a note saying "Free to deploy the Guard; Court is on our side."

9:00 a.m. - Marina City Dock - Chicago River

Lake Michigan was in a bad mood. This morning it was all whitecaps with that cold November air that rips through clothing and chills you to the bone. The same wind that was churning up the Lake also put them on it as it was deemed too risky to fly Rockefeller all the way in on the Black Hawk. Instead, they put down and picked up a boat in Gary, Indiana. The last 30 miles over the Lake were nauseating, even for an experienced sailor. By the time the Galeon 450 nosed in a slip under the Marina Towers, everyone on board was a bit green.

Tracy Rockefeller stepped out from the wheelhouse in a dark coat zipped to her chin with a baseball hat pulled down over her eyes. Delaware, Kathy Curtis was on the dock to meet her. After a quick informal greeting, Kathy turned to the boat's captain and crew and stated, please stick around, we might need you for evac. My team can take it from here. Tracy also turned, held her hand up, and signaled she was in agreement.

Curtis then turned to Rockefeller stating, "Slight change of plans, we will do the interview upstairs here at Smith & Wollensky. It's the easiest and safest option. Once we are finished, it's a very short walk over to the Wrigley Building where we have a podium and security set up. Plan is still to fly you back out but it's dependent on the wind dying down at least a bit. We have cleared the square across the street from the Wrigley Building so we are going to try to bring the Black Hawk in there."

They moved along the dock into the restaurant's service entrance. Upstairs, the dining room was closed but lit—the floor to ceiling windows rattled in the gusts. A producer from ABC was waiting by the bar and led them to a table by the window, the river churning angrily below. Once Rockefeller was seated, Curtis walked back over to the ABC producer and stated, "just want to make sure there are no misunderstandings, this doesn't air until Rockefeller is out of Chicago. Otherwise, her security could be compromised."

Chris Gannon introduced himself and handed Rockefeller a small wireless clip-on mic. As they were making final adjustment to the lighting and camera angles, Gannon turned to Rockefeller:

Gannon: "Mrs. Rockefeller, did you see the President's interview on FOX & Friends this morning?"

Rockefeller: "I didn't but an aide handed me a transcript of it. He's really lost the plot."

Gannon: "Can we dive into that?"

Rockefeller: "That's why I'm here."

The producer signed that they were ready, and the red recording light on the camera blinked.

Gannon: "Good morning, I'm here with Governor Rockefeller. Governor, the President this morning not only repeated his claims of voter fraud, but this time indicated that you and the Rockefeller family were deeply involved and helped fund it. The President said he's got evidence that he will be sharing with the American people in a few days."

Rockefeller turned directly towards the camera: "To start, there is no evidence anywhere that anyone has produced of voter fraud. America's elections are the gold standard of security and integrity. The President fears that he's lost the election and the only way he has a hope of holding onto power is to have it nullified. As for some mythical deep state trying to buy an election, based on the President's own public statements, he is far richer than any of the Rockefellers at this point. It's been a very long time since a Rockefeller was on the Forbes 400 list. And for the record: I married into the family—I wasn't born a Rockefeller, James and I were only married for two years and that was a very long time ago. Growing up, my family was very solidly middle class. Things were tight. Both my parents worked and I helped put myself through college."

Gannon: "And as for the President's claim that you have been in hiding?"

Rockefeller: "I guess that makes me the first person in history to hide out in a Smith & Wollensky's. I'm also not sure how he squares the several public interviews I have given in the last few days with being in hiding? If anything, it's more a question that should be asked of him. Other than a few taped interviews from the Oval Office, he hasn't been sighted in public since the week before election day."

Gannon: "So what should the country do now?"

Turning back to Gannon, Rockefeller replied: "It's really quite simple Chris. Allow all the votes to be counted. Then we'll all see who has won. That's how our democracy works."

Gannon's producer signaled cut, what they had just recorded was pure gold.

9:00 a.m. - Michigan Avenue - Chicago

That morning, the Prairie Boys had been pouring into the park in waves. After days of waiting, they felt their moment was now. Flags waving, militia patches proudly displayed, cheap body armor buckled tight, and walkie-talkies clipped to belts, they were ready to go. Word of the President's call-in on FOX had spun them up into a near frenzy. Faces raw from the wind, they were anxious to get moving.

At 9:30 a.m., the man they referred to as "Sergeant" climbed up onto a couple of stacked crates, "Men", he shouted, "we are going to march south down Michigan Avenue, cross the Chicago River and then head over to city hall to secure the voting machines and ballots that are being stored there. Anyone gets in our way, take them out. Now move out!"

Three quarters of a mile away, a very different crowd gathered in Wrigley Plaza, spilling out onto Michigan Ave. Word had gone out that the Governor was planning on making an appearance and would be making a few statements on the election. It was a mix of professionals, tourists, and students from the nearby University of Chicago business school that South Carolina, Jennifer Remington had organized. The DuSable Bridge had been closed to traffic and squad cars had blocked off Michigan Ave south of Ohio Street.

At 9:30 a.m., Tracy Rockefeller came out the main door of the Wrigley Building with Governor Kathy Curtis by her side. A phalanx of State Troopers followed behind. As they walked towards the podium, the troopers spread out in front of the crowd on either side. Word immediately went through the crowd that Governor Rockefeller was there, and a hundred different cell phones started live streaming the event.

Rockefeller spoke for ten minutes, finishing her speech by thanking local election workers by name.

The clapping hadn't finished when Curtis's head of security received an urgent code red alert: "*Militia moving south on Michigan Ave. Just passed Delaware.*"

Curtis squeezed Tracy's elbow and whispered, "We need to go now." At exactly the same moment, the black handset they both had in their pockets rang. They both crouched down behind the podium and answered. It was Bell.

Bell: We are on top of the situation. Boat is already on its way from Marina Towers. It will be down at the Wrigley building dock in one minute. I want you both on it. Kathy, leave your security detail behind and tell them to get the crowd across the street and into the Apple store. Put the Troopers in front. They will be safe there. Black Hawk will meet you at the bottom of South Pier and pick up Tracy. Kathy, you can then double back, and the boat will drop you off at Union Station. Have your security meet you there."

Curtis then turned to her head of security; "Get everyone off of Michigan Ave. Tell them to go into the Apple Store across the street. Open up DuSable Bridge, I want to let the mob through. Get a detail to meet me at Union Station in 10 minutes."

Word of Rockefeller's appearance had now reached the Prairie Boys. They became a wall of noise and chaos rushing down Michigan Ave chanting, "*lock her up!*" The militia hit a phalanx of Chicago police in riot gear at Ohio Street just as Rockefeller and Curtis stepped onto the boat. The line held, shields locked together like modern legionaries, as tear gas canisters whistled overhead. From out of the middle of the mob, a pair of Molotov cocktails sailed over the line of shields, exploding on the pavement and engulfing several riot policemen in flames. From the same spot, two shots rang out and two more policemen crumpled to the ground grasping at their legs. From the roof of the Intercontinental Hotel, a police sniper, clicked his radio and said, "shots fired, I have eyes on the shooters, can I take the shot?" At that moment, the line broke and the militia started to surge through. As the crowd surged, a voice came back on the radio, "weapons tight, engage on positive ID." The sniper responded, "ID is positive" and then in rapid succession, two bodies crumpled to the ground on Michigan Avenue, their owners suddenly discovering the shortcomings of mail order body armor.

As the second body crumpled, word rushed through the crowd that "Sergeant" was down. The surge forward stopped as confusion took hold. It was just enough time for the Chicago riot police to regroup, retreat to the side streets, and pull their wounded to safety.

As soon as both Rockefeller and Curtis were on board, the Galeon 450 raced up the Chicago River, breaking every "no wake" rule along the way. As they approached the bottom of the South Pier, the Black Hawk was settling onto its skids. The Galeon 450 pulled alongside the pier, stopping just long enough for Rockefeller and one security guard to jump off and run towards the helipad. As the boat pulled away and did a 360-degree turn, Curtis saw the two climbing on board and the Black Hawk beginning to lift off. As they headed back down the

Chicago River, Curtis could just make out the two Apaches as they dropped into formation on either side of the Black Hawk. With it came a sense of relief as she knew Bell had them covered the whole time.

On the Black Hawk, Rockefeller's handset rang again. It was Bell.

Bell: "Glad you are safe. I'd like you to come to Washington DC now. I will arrange for Elle to be brought in from the Lodge to meet you here. I think we are going to need you in the Capital tomorrow."

Rockefeller: "Harry, that was too close for comfort. I will need a glass of wine when I get to DC."

Bell: "Yes, but it will be hugely impactful. I'll go put a bottle on ice now."

As soon as Bell was off the line with Rockefeller, he dialed Julia Jackson's number.

As soon as he heard her pick up he said, "It's Harry, I think it's time to put the word out that Hawley Oil's loans have been called and it's facing bankruptcy. Can you leak it through FOX?"

Jackson: "Consider it done."

10:00 a.m. – Floor - House of Representatives

The galleries were empty. McCollins had banned all visitors today and ordered the C-SPAN cameras off.

McCollins banged the gavel; the room silenced. "House will come to order—"

Fitzwilliams stood. "I am introducing a motion to vacate the chair."

Representative Jim Livingstone of Texas immediately followed: "Motion to Table."

McCollins then called for a vote. The chamber fell silent.

Five minutes later, the clerk read the tally 210 for, 225 against.

McCollins felt like he had been punched in the gut.

Fitzwilliams stood again. "Before we proceed, I would like to read you a letter George Washington wrote as he neared the end of his 2nd term. This letter was given to a friend of his and that man's ancestor passed it to me last night. This is the first time it has been read in public."

Fitzwilliams unfolded the vellum and held it up briefly. Those directly behind him could see Washington's signature and a gasp went through the chamber.

Fitzwilliams started: "Our Nation is forever fragile, dependent on the honor and sacrifices of men to survive…

When he was finished, the house remained completely silent. The message and warning clear as the day. Slowly from the back, a single set of hands started clapping. It was infectious. Within seconds, the chamber had erupted in applause.

When it finally started to die down, Fitzwilliams spoke softly into the mic and said, "Let us be worthy of their sacrifices and dreams."

The roll call took ten minutes. Ayes swamped the Nays. When the final number flashed, the House was briefly, shockingly, quiet. McCollins stared at the board as if it were his death warrant. "He'll kill me," he whispered. "He'll kill me, he'll kill me—" The whisper ratcheted to a scream. McCollins's Chief of Staff came forward and tried to calm him; he flailed; the Capitol Police finally called medics. McCollins went out on a gurney, eyes wild, yelling the President's name and acting like a man possessed.

Once McCollins was out and the chamber had a few minutes to recover its composure, the Speaker Pro Tempore hammered it back into session. "The chair recognizes the gentlewoman from Massachusetts."

Martha Woodall stepped forward, "I would like to nominate Samuel Fitzwilliams of Illinois."

When the voting was over, it was a landslide. Only 55 of McCollins and Hawley's hardcore followers voted against Fitzwilliams.

The chamber erupted again in applause.

Fifteen minutes later, the news was being carried on all the major networks.

In a townhouse a short walk away, Bell turned to Nate Burr, "Hawley's now mortally wounded. He just doesn't know it yet. Can you please draft up articles of impeachment. We will need them for tomorrow."

11:30 a.m. - Ops Room - Raven Rock

Clark stood next to Hawley. The bank of monitors on the wall all had the same headlines scrolling across the bottom of the screens, cutting across the video from the riot in Chicago:

McCollins out as Speaker of the House, Fitzwilliams elected new Speaker.

Followed by:

Rockefeller challenges Hawley: Allow all the votes to be counted. Then we'll all see who has won.

And finally:

Hawley Oil is facing bankruptcy

Hawley was quivering with anger. "Get me Bragg," he said.

An aide grabbed a secure line and put the call into the Chairman's office at the Pentagon.

"General," Hawley hissed, "I want the Guard deployed to every voting and tallying site in the country. They are to secure all voting machines and ballots and ship them to Fort Belvoir. Anyone who interferes is to be considered an enemy combatant and treated as such."

Bragg: "Understood, but please also transmit in writing to make sure there is no misunderstanding on intent."

Hawley: "Fine, but you're just looking to cover your miserable ass."

Hawley dropped the phone back onto the receiver and turned to Clark: "Draft and send under the President's authority as commander in chief. Once you are done with that, issue an arrest warrant for Tracy Rockefeller for treason and election interference. Also call Cohen at Treasury. Tell him to shut the markets and to keep them shut until this is all over. I need to know who is behind Mount Vernon LLC!"

Clark: "What shall we do about McCollins? He looks like he is having a breakdown."

Hawley: "Nothing, he is of no use to us now. Release the Guard order and the Rockefeller arrest warrant to the press at 1:00 p.m."

Jimmy Walsh was at his station in the back corner. He didn't hear the whole conversation, but he clearly heard the order to arrest Tracy Rockefeller.

Noon - The Townhouse - Washington D.C.

Bell was sitting in his private office, contemplating Hawley's fate. While he knew the final decision would ultimately rest on his shoulders, the gravity of it demanded input, discussion, and alignment among a number of the Guarantors and Hoyt. He picked up the secure handset and conferenced in Burr, Lewis, Damon, Hoyt, Jackson, Taylor, Tyler and Teruel.

"We need to settle on what to ultimately do with Hawley. We can't try him," Bell said. "Hard for that not to turn into a circus. Prison turns him into a rallying point. A bullet turns him into a saint or martyr. Exile seems like the least bad option."

"Exile without trial," Susan Lewis said. "Do you have any idea what that sounds like, this isn't ancient Rome?"

"Feels a bit like tyranny," Julia Jackson said. "Which is exactly what we are trying to avoid"

"We are not killing him," Taylor said. "And we are not leaving him where he can do future damage, those are my parameters. If anyone has a better solution than exile, I'm listening."

Lewis' voice cut in. "What about a truth commission? Immunity for testimony, full disclosure?"

"And then what?" Burr cut in. "He writes a book, does a repentance tour, starts a podcast, shows up on FOX every Sunday."

Hoyt finally spoke up, "Washington's fourth rule," he said quietly, tapping the vellum. "The Guarantors act only when the Constitution is threatened. Fifth: remove the threat, then return power." He lifted his gaze. "It does not say we have to make a public example. It does not say we have to satisfy anyone's sense of catharsis."

"It also doesn't say we get to make people vanish," Lewis said.

"No," Hoyt agreed. "But it does tell us to remove the threat, which exile does satisfy."

Teruel spoke up, "we have the resources, and I can handle the arrangements."

"This still feels hugely uncomfortable" Jackson asked.

"As Harry said, it's the least bad," Teruel replied. "Certainly, more humane than a bullet in the back of the head...or how Gaddafi went."

"Look," Bell said, "if we give him a show trial, we blow gasoline on an already burning country. If we just let him walk, we invite the next Hawley. Washington didn't give us that luxury, the decree is very clear on "*remove*"."

Hoyt then cut in, "leaving him on the board is most dangerous thing we can do."

Tyler finally asked, "Can we do it and still sleep?"

"Can we sleep if we don't?" Bell said. "Are we aligned on exile?"

One by one, they all said yes.

After Lewis gave the final yes, Bell said, "Good, John and I will arrange it."

12:15 p.m. - Base Commander's Office - Norfolk Naval Station

Taylor picked up the secure line on the first ring. The display behind the phone lit up with "Chairman of the Joint Chiefs of Staff" but Taylor already knew who it would be.

Bragg started: "General Taylor, I have a direct order from the President. You are to deploy the National Guard to every voting and tallying site nationwide. They are to secure all voting machines and ballots and ship them to Fort Belvoir. Anyone who interferes is to be considered an enemy combatant. This order is effective immediately."

Taylor responded: "Confirmed, order has been received. Given its extraordinary nature, I will need to run this by The Judge Advocate General before executing."

Bragg: "Understood."

Taylor: "I will revert if there are any concerns."

1:00 p.m. – The Townhouse - Washington D.C.

Elle and Tracy Rockefeller had just arrived. Fitzwilliams, Burr, Lockwood, and Bell were already seated around the large conference table. A bank of TV monitors lined the wall, all blinking with flash updates as Hawley's latest moves hit the wires.

Bell picked up a handset and dialed Taylor.

Bell: "Charles, you are on speaker, has Bragg pushed the order down?"

Taylor: "He has, I've bought a bit of time by insisting on JAG review. We probably have until 3 p.m. until Hawley starts firing people."

Bell: "Can you have all Raven Rock communications blocked or routed to your command?"

Taylor: "Military, command and control, probably. You would still need to block cell and sat phones separately."

Bell: "See if you can do it right after midnight. If you need help, reach out to Teruel. He would know where the backdoor is"

Taylor: "Will do."

Burr leaned forward: "§ 592 and 593 clearly negate the order. Hawley is probably impeachable now under 595 and for a few other things.

Taylor: "I will pass that The Judge Advocate General, I'm sure he will see it the same way we are.

Rockefeller spoke next: "What do we do about this arrest warrant, he's gone so far as to even threaten my broader family?"

Burr: "As soon as it's issued, we will challenge it on a probable cause basis. Same for any others that might come out of Clark's Justice Department."

Bell: "You mentioned Elle got a text from an agent of Hawley's detail."

Elle Rockefeller: "I did. He's one of my ex's but we have remained on good terms. It said: *hope you and your mother are safe. I'm at Raven Rock with the President. Things here are getting very weird.*"

Bell: "Please text him back: I'm safe and with friends. Might need your help but need to know if you are on my mother's or Hawley's side."

Elle: "Done."

Bell: "Let me know if you get a reply."

Bell then turned to Lockwood and asked, "Walter, shall we open the Court back up?"

Lockwood: "It's time. Charles, can you have your men clear out the rest of the militia members?"

Taylor: "Consider it done. My last report indicated that half had left on their own accord anyway. They weren't happy about being stripped of weapons and photographed. What's the situation. In Chicago? From the video I've seen it looks messy."

Bell: "I just spoke to Kathy. Chicago Police are rounding up the last of the militia members as we speak. Four policemen were injured, two with burns, two with gunshot wounds, but none are in critical condition. Two militia members were shot and killed. As for the militia that was headed into Los Angeles, somehow, they ended up in Compton. Not sure how to put this, but the locals are taking care of that problem."

Rockefeller: "Where are we with the States?"

Bell: "Hawley's down to 8 with the Governors still openly backing him. The 2 Dakotas, Wyoming, Idaho, Louisiana, Mississippi, Arkansas, and Texas. Texas is the main concern, the Governor there, Ross Hogg, is closely tied to Hawley and we believe working hard behind the scenes to keep Louisiana, Mississippi, and Arkansas on board."

Elle Rockefeller: "I just got a response, "I'm on your side," followed by: "I saw the warrant they're drafting, they're coming for her, Elle."

Bell: "That may come in quite useful. Can we talk later?"

Elle: "Of course."

Bell: "In terms of next steps, Walter, please get back to the Court. Please remind Hoyt to pocket this morning's ruling. He also needs to move on Bomgardner right before 3 p.m. When the ruling does not come out at 3 p.m., Hawley will figure out he's been had and we need

Bomgardner off the table before then. Sam, call the House back into session tomorrow morning. Please reach out to Webster and ask for the same for the Senate. Nate Burr will deliver the articles of impeachment to you at the house right before you open the session. The sooner you get them voted on, the sooner they can be passed to John and the Senate for the trial. We will need to impeach both Hawley and Harris back to back. We have Harris on treason as he issued the orders to the militias. Ideally, we have this all wrapped up by mid-afternoon. Tracy, you and Elle should plan on staying here tonight. Also, Susan Lewis has finally been able to get out of New York City. She will be joining us here later this afternoon. Let's regroup around 4 p.m.

Everyone nodded and started to head out. Just as the two Rockefellers were about to leave, Bell's cell phone rang. Caller ID came up, John Cohen, Secretary of Treasury. Bell waved the two Rockefellers' back into the room as he placed his cell in the middle of the table, answered the call and hit speaker.

Bell: "Hi John, it's Harry, what can I do for you?'

Cohen: "Harry, a transfer from your bank came up in a deep search we are doing for the President."

Bell: "John, we move billions of dollars every day, can you give me a few more details?"

Cohen: "It's related to Hawley Oil."

Bell: "I wasn't aware Hawley Oil was a customer of ours."

Cohen: "It isn't, it's related to the story you might have seen on the news."

Bell: "Speaking of the news, have you seen what happened in the House this morning?"

Cohen: "Of course, that was really unexpected."

Bell: "I gave Fitzwilliams that letter. John, we have known each other for a long time, you don't want to end up on the wrong side of this."

Cohen: "Understood, thanks."

The line went dead, and with it any hope Hawley had of finding out who was behind Mount Vernon LLC.

Bell turned and smiled. Elle Rockefeller sat wide eyed, and Tracy just nodded.

2:50 p.m. - Chief Justice's Office - Supreme Court

Chief Justice Hoyt got up from behind the table in the small private conference room off his office that he preferred to use when reviewing cases. He had already tapped the buzzer under the table to summon John, the Sergeant at Arms. Before he even got halfway across his vast official office, John was tapping on his door, with two lieutenants flanking him on either side. Hoyt opened the door and stepped into the hallway, quickly nodding and saying, "follow me."

A short walk down the hall brought them to Associate Justice Bomgardner's office. Hoyt didn't bother to knock; he simply walked in with his three companions trailing behind. Bomgardner was caught by surprise. He had been standing by the window, watching the DC Guard mop up the few remaining Mountain Men. The metal security shutters over the windows had been raised a few minutes before. Whatever fight the Mountain Men had in them initially, 24 hours out in the wet cold November DC weather with little food and no sleep had sucked it

161

out of them. As Bomgardner turned to face Hoyt, Hoyt turned around to John and ordered, "take Justice Bomgardner down to join Justice Coney. Relieve him of all of his electronic devices." Before Bomgardner could even protest, Hoyt stepped through the door and back into the hallway. As soon as he was clear of the door, Hoyt picked up his cell phone and called his chief clerk, "Eric, this morning's ruling, pocket it and then delete all references off the system. As far as we are concerned, it never happened."

3:15 p.m. - Presidential Suite Sitting Room - Raven Rock

Hawley, Clark, and Harris were sitting around the coffee table watching the bank of monitors on the wall. As the minutes tumbled by, Hawley was becoming increasing agitated again.

Hawley finally turning to Clark and hissed, "Where's the Supreme Court ruling supporting my invocation of the Insurrection Act?"

Clark: "It should have been released at 3:00 p.m. That's what Bomgardner promised."

Hawley: "Get that idiot on the phone."

Clark, dialing Bomgardner: "There's no answer, he usually picks up immediately."

Hawley: "Fuck, we are being played. Why am I not seeing pictures of Guard Troops moving into voting centers on the media feeds. That order went out hours ago."

Hawley, picking up the secure line to Bragg at the Pentagon: "General, I gave you a direct order hours ago, why has it not been implemented?"

Bragg: "Mr. President, as you are aware, I have no direct command authority over any units. I passed on your order to General Taylor. Given its extraordinary nature, he requested The Judge Advocate General review the legality of the order before implementing."

Hawley: "If I don't hear that troops are moving in the next half hour, I am firing you, then Taylor, then anyone else who gets in my way. Have I made myself clear?"

Bragg: "Yes sir, I will let General Taylor know."

Hawley turning to Clark: "Get back to DC. I want that arrest warrant out for Rockefeller tonight. Have every FBI agent in the country out looking for her."

Harris then asked: "any word on McCollins?"

Clark: "He's at Walter Reed Hospital, heavily sedated."

Hawley, turning to Harris: "Call Hogg in Texas. Find out what the Texas Guard is doing and who they are taking orders from."

3:30 p.m. - Base Commander's Office - Norfolk Naval Station

Bragg's call came through right about when Taylor expected it to.

Bragg: "I just got off with the President. I'm sure you can guess how the call went. He thinks you are stalling."

Taylor: "We both know what he has ordered is wildly wrong."

Bragg: "He has threatened to fire both of us if troops are not moving in the next half hour."

Taylor: "We both know he can't fire us for refusing to follow an illegal order."

Bragg: "I don't think he cares about legal niceties at this point."

Taylor: "Hawley might not but the rest of the nation does. History will judge us both on how we handle the next 24 hours."

Bragg: "Send me the JAG ruling as soon as you get it."

Taylor: "It just landed in my inbox and I will forward. Scanning it quickly, it's as expected. Clear violation of § 592 and 593. Just got a separate note from TJAG, he says he called his former classmate, Associate Justice Walter Lockwood just to confirm his reading of the law. Lockwood concurred, so any challenge Hawley might try isn't going anywhere."

Bragg: "Well, I better go work on my resume."

4:00 p.m. - Main Lounge - The Lodge

Susan Lewis and John Teruel had just arrived and joined the group in the Lounge. The setting sun was bringing warmth into the room. The atmosphere felt lighter, as if the darkness of the last few days was finally lifting. The monitors on the walls, scrolling with the latest events from around the country. Shots of National Guard troops in Texas still occupying polling sites, the Mountain Men being cleared from the Supreme Court, street battles in Compton, the steel shutters on the Supreme Court being raised, cell phone footage showing the end of Fitzwilliams speech and McCollins leaving on a gurney. All the monitors were muted but the messages were all very clear.

Bell started the meeting by conferencing Taylor, Lockwood, McLean, Curtis, and Jackson in.

Bell: "Charles, have you heard back from Bragg?"

Taylor: "Just did. Hawley is threatening to fire both of us if his orders aren't implemented. I have the ruling from TJAG declaring them illegal so when he calls, I will push back hard. At this point, I am highly confident in the loyalty of my chain of command. Just let me know how you want this played out."

Bell: "We are going to go ahead and cut all of Hawley's secure command and control communications at midnight. Teruel's here. His people did all the upgrades to Raven Rocks C2 systems and security a few years back. They know where the back door is so they will take care of it. We are also going to need a Special Ops team to hit Raven Rock tomorrow. Can you organize?"

Taylor: "I can, just give me the time, objective, and rules of engagement."

Bell: "Objective #1 is to get Hawley out, in our custody, and alive. We should take all efforts to minimize casualties. Most of the people with him are innocents. See if you can get your team there and on the ground before dawn. Have them grab anyone who comes topside."

Taylor: "Clear, given the sensitivity, I might borrow a team from our friends at Langley for this. They all used to work for me and understand confidentiality."

Bell, turning back to Teruel: "Let's cut all of Hawley's communications and jam cell and satellite transmissions as of midnight. I need one line left open. Elle – please give John Jimmy Walsh's cell phone number. Jimmy is going to help us get Hawley out of Raven Rock."

Lockwood came on the line: "Hoyt has taken care of Bomgardner, but we do need to decide what we want to do with both of them."

Bell: "At the end of the day it's Hoyt's call but my recommendation would be to officially keep Coney and Bomgardner on the court for now but neutered. Bomgardner will retire in 6 months with Coney to follow a year later. Otherwise, it looks like our nation's highest court was politically compromised and corrupt. The country will need to heal once this is done and taking them both out now will not help that process. If Hoyt agrees with this approach, I will have Burr go over and meet with both and impress upon them what their situation truly is and options are. If they aren't willing to go along, its impeachment and a long jail sentence. Neither will do well in a Federal Prison."

Lewis leaned forward, clasping Fitzwilliams' hand warmly: "Congratulations Sam, that was a brilliant speech this morning."

Fitzwilliams, smiling: "Lots of practice with pregame locker room speeches."

Bell: "Susan, tomorrow we are going to impeach both Hawley and Harris. Plan is to start with impeachment proceeding in the House at 9 a.m. and then move to the trial in the Senate at 1 p.m. If we do this right, it will all be wrapped up by 3 p.m. Nate Burr's going to deliver the impeachment articles to Sam right before 9 a.m. He will also have information packets for each member of the House and the Senate detailing the evidence against Hawley."

Fitzwilliams: If we impeach both Hawley and Harris, won't that result in my becoming the President as the next in line?"

Bell: "That's where the next part of the plan comes in. I believe vote tallying has resumed in most of the country. Bill McLean and Kathy Curtis are going to work with their fellow governors to get as much of the vote counted by 3 p.m. tomorrow as they can. Julia Jackson, please make sure all the major networks cover this and report the tallies as they are released. Lynn Tyler and George Damon, get on the networks and do interviews supporting the count. Based on all the exit polls I've seen, Tracy won by a considerable margin. If we can get enough of the count in, Tracy should be able to declare victory legitimately by tomorrow afternoon. Once that happens, plan to have Congress declare Rockefeller as the acting President until the official Inauguration Day on January 20th. Sam this way you don't have to resign your seat and go down as the shortest serving Speaker in history."

Rockefeller: "What is the plan for Hawley, Harris, and Clark?"

Bell: "The first two are going to disappear. Burr is going to take care of Clark. Washington left very clear instructions on how those that try to seize power should be treated."

The room went silent.

5:00 p.m. - Replica Oval Office - Raven Rock

Hawley sat in the room alone looking at his reflection in the monitors on the far wall. He was a man used to being in complete control of his environment but now, for reasons he did not understand, it was all slipping away. It was as if an unknown foe was slowing peeling away his authority. His supreme ego and self-confidence were suddenly cracking, he felt small and confined. Hawley picked up the secure line and punched the button for Bragg.

Hawley: "Why haven't I seen troop movements?"

Bragg: "Mr. President, The Judge Advocate General determined that the order was illegal."

Hawley: "You're fired."

Bragg: "Sir, I cannot be removed for refusing to follow an order that has been determined to be illegal."

Hawley: "I'm replacing you with Taylor."

Bragg: "Taylor shares the same position."

Hawley: "Fine, I will fire him too."

Bragg: "Mr. President, you have the right to appeal the TJAG ruling to the Supreme Court, but unless the court overturns TJAG ruling, neither one of us, nor any of our subordinates will relinquish their commands."

Hawley: "I'm releasing the files on your little misadventure in the Middle East. You are finished."

Bragg: "Go ahead Mr. President. I have already sent them to Speaker Fitzwilliams and Senate Majority Leader Webster."

Hawley: "You're an asshole."

Hawley, shaking in anger, got up from behind the desk and walked to the door. As he opened it, Harris was walking by in the hallway.

Hawley: "Did you get ahold of Hogg?"

Harris: "I did, he said nothing is going on. Texas Guard is still taking orders from him. They have had no orders or communication from anyone at the Pentagon."

Hawley: "I need to go think."

and then he disappeared down the hallway towards the Presidential Quarters.

Day 6 – The Bill Comes Due
12:01 a.m. - Main Control Room - Raven Rock

The yellow warning light on the wall started flashing. The monitors indicated all communication lines were down. At first the staff assumed this was a test or drill. After five minutes, when the lines weren't restored, panic began to set in. One aide, while frantically flipping switches, checked his cell phone and yelled that he no longer had a signal.

In the corner cubicle, Jimmy Walsh pulled his cell phone out. It showed five bars of reception. His body tensed as he knew now that more was to come.

4:00 a.m. - Raven Rock Mountain

Special Operations Group (SOG) slowly spread across Raven Rock Mountain. Traditionally, the CIA's Special Operations Group is responsible for covert operations that the U.S. government does not want to be overtly associated with, and this certainly qualified. The Group Commander had served under General Charles Taylor, and it was a call from Taylor that had landed him command of SOG when he retired from the Army. SOG, more than any other unit in the vast U.S. military intelligence universe, understood "need to know." Their orders were simple: secure all the entrances and exits on Raven Rock, take into custody anyone who emerges. If engaged, you may return fire.

7:00 a.m. - The Chief Justice's Chambers - U.S. Supreme Court

Hoyt ushered Burr in as soon as he arrived. A pot of fresh, hot coffee had just been placed on the coffee table in front of the facing couches.

Burr: "Did Harry or Walter talk to you last night on our suggested approach for Coney and Bomgardner?"

Hoyt: "He did, and I am quite happy to have you handle it, thanks."

Burr: "Good. Shall we do it here? That way there are no misunderstandings."

Hoyt: "Not my first choice, but probably the most expedient. I'll ask John to bring them up."

Hoyt walked to the door, opened it, and had a brief discussion with the Sergeant at Arms. Five minutes later, Coney and Bomgardner were ushered into his office. As they arrived, Hoyt pointed to the small conference room on the side and they all filed in, Burr closing the door behind the group. Coney's eyes were filled with dread and guilt; Bomgardner remained defiant.

Hoyt: "I'll cut to the chase. Mr. Burr is here to lay out your options. This is not a discussion or negotiation. You will have to make a choice, and then there is no going back."

Burr: "Ginny and Samuel, you have three options, and you both have to agree on which one to take. Option #1 is you both will die in a car accident this afternoon. Your bodies will lie in state in the Capitol, and you will be given an official funeral with military honors.

"Option #2 is you walk out of here this afternoon and try your luck with the justice system. We will have you immediately arrested, and you will be put on trial. Should you be found guilty, which is a near certain outcome, you will then spend the rest of your life in federal prison.

"Option #3 is you will stay on the Court—Samuel, you for six months, and Ginny, you for eighteen. During that period, you will vote the way Chief Justice Hoyt instructs you to. You will ask no questions and will not participate in deliberations. You will make no public appearances or give any speeches. At the end of that period, you will resign your seat for health reasons, leave Washington, D.C., and fade into obscurity. You will write no books, give no lectures, or make any attempt to reenter public life. Should you violate any of these terms, you will not live to see out the day. I will give you fifteen minutes to think about it."

Burr and Hoyt then rose, exited the small conference room, and shut the door behind them.

Hoyt: "Another cup of coffee, Nate?"

Burr: "That would be lovely."

Five minutes later the door to the conference room opened. Coney and Bomgardner walked over to where the other two were seated. Bomgardner said simply, "Option 3." Coney nodded in agreement.

Burr: "You understand that the terms are ironclad and not open to any future modification."

Coney: "We do."

Burr: "Anthony, looks like we have an agreement. Please keep them in the basement holding room until the rest of this has blown over."

Hoyt: "Happy to. I will have John return them to their cells."

And with that Burr got up, shook Hoyt's hand goodbye, and opened the door. As he did so, the Sergeant at Arms arrived.

8:00 a.m. - Attorney General's Office - Department of Justice

Burr walked straight into the Attorney General's suite. It was the type of office set up to intimidate. Dark wood paneling covered the walls; the curtains opened just enough to let strips of light in. Clark sat behind the massive partners desk at the far end. He did not rise when Burr entered. He simply waved his hand toward one of the barrel chairs in front of the desk. Neither man attempted any pleasantries.

Clark: "Mr. Burr, I assume you are here to discuss Mrs. Rockefeller's surrender."

Burr: "Mr. Clark, yes, it's related to Mrs. Rockefeller. Here are our terms."

Burr slid a folder across the desk. It contained call logs, transcripts, bank statements, photographs, a witness proffer, and a draft indictment with Clark's name on the top.

Clark opened the folder and started flipping through it. His face went sheet white.

Burr leaned forward and said quietly, "Chief Justice Hoyt, Speaker of the House Fitzwilliams, and Senate Majority Leader Webster all have identical copies."

Clark put down the folder and leaned back in the chair, still defiant.

Clark: "I'm the Attorney General; no one would dare file an indictment against me. If anyone tried, the President would fire them immediately."

Burr: "That is true. However, Hawley will not be President by dusk, and neither will you be the Attorney General. Let me tell you how today is going to go and what role you are going to play. This morning, the House of Representatives is going to impeach both Hawley and Harris. The Senate trial will follow almost immediately.

"As both the Attorney General and Hawley's long-term personal lawyer, you will represent the President at the Senate trial. Once the evidence of Hawley and Harris is presented, you will not dispute the facts, other than to say the President does not believe he has done anything wrong. At the conclusion of the trial, you will return to this office and immediately resign. You will then leave Washington, D.C., and fade into obscurity. You will never practice law again, make a public appearance, or give a speech. You will write no books, give no lectures, or make any attempt to reenter public life. Should you violate any of these terms, you will not live to see out the day.

"If you do not cooperate, you will be put on trial and your entire vile existence laid out in front of the entire nation. You will die alone in a cold jail cell."

Clark, shaking and barely able to speak, his world suddenly turned upside down:

Clark: "What time do I need to be at the Senate?"

Burr: "Be there by 1:00 p.m."

Clark, still trembling as Burr was getting up to leave:

Clark: "Who are you people?"

Burr: "None of your fucking business."

8:00 a.m. - Presidential Quarters - Raven Rock

Hawley had not slept well at all. He spent most of the night tossing and turning. By 8:00

a.m. he gave up trying and decided to get up. He grabbed his bathrobe and opened the door into

the study where an aide had already delivered his morning coffee and pastries. After pouring

himself a cup, he clicked the remote to turn on the wall of monitors. Nothing but static filled

every screen. Angry and confused, he rushed down to the main command center. Upon arrival,

Hawley shouted at the duty officer.

Hawley: "What's happened with our communications?"

Duty Officer: "They have been down since midnight. We are working on it, but it seems

like our fiber optic trunk line has been cut."

Hawley: "And cell?"

Duty Officer: "Also down. Cell towers probably use the same lines."

Hawley: "Satellite?"

Duty Officer: "Dishes are unresponsive. As soon as it is full daylight, we will send a team

up to investigate."

Hawley: "Get them up there now!"

Hawley, feeling like a hunted animal, turned and headed back toward the Presidential

Quarters. As he passed the Vice President's suite, he stopped and decided to go in. The lounge area was still pitch black as he walked across to the bedroom door. Hawley didn't bother knocking; he just pulled it open, let it slam against the wall, and flicked on the light. Harris sat bolt upright, another different aide, naked beside him. She looked up, shocked and terrified.

Hawley: "Lily, don't bother, I've known you were fucking him for years. Stay. Joe, I'm going to have your dick bronzed when this is done. Our communications have been down since midnight. I need you to get up there and find out what's going on. Now!"

Hawley then flipped the light back off and headed back to his suite to try and figure out what was happening.

8:45 a.m. - Speaker's Office - Capitol Building

The door to Fitzwilliams' office was open. Burr strode right in, carrying a large leather bag in his right hand filled with the evidence folders against Hawley and Harris.

Burr, as he dropped the bag on a side table: "Morning, Mr. Speaker. Your new surroundings suit you well, Sam."

Fitzwilliams, smiling: "Thanks, Nate. I've got Martha Woodall lined up to introduce the impeachment resolution. Once she does, I will immediately move to have the full House consider it based on the evidence they all will have received. We should have it all wrapped up by noon, if not sooner."

Burr: "Excellent. I've also asked Senate Majority Leader Webster to leak it to his quorum that this is happening. You will likely have most of the Senate watching from the gallery. I've also arranged for the Senators to be given the evidence packets upon arrival. This will expedite the debate when we get to the other side of the Capitol this afternoon. I will be in the gallery for the duration. If you hit any roadblocks, call a short recess and I will meet you in your office."

Fitzwilliams: "Thanks, Nate. The sooner this is over the better."

9:00 a.m. - Raven Rock

Harris took the main elevator up to the entrance level on his own. When the elevator door finally opened, he stepped into a vast empty room. The large steel blast doors were firmly shut and there were no guards in sight. As he didn't know how to operate the doors on his own, he decided to go back into the service area and find one of the emergency stairwells to the surface. He climbed the three flights of stairs, cursing Hawley under his breath. At the top, he flipped the security override switch and hit the red "open" button.

The large steel door slowly opened to the gray, cold November day. Harris stepped out onto the pine needles covering the forest floor, reached for his cell phone, and his world went black.

The SOG officer removed the syringe from Harris' neck and pulled the body into the brush. His partner checked that no one was coming up the stairs behind Harris, then quietly shut the stairwell door. The SOG officer hit the transmit button on his secure comms and stated, "Prisoner secured, believe it might be VP Harris. Please advise."

Immediately the SOG Commander replied, "Transport down to command base and then return to your position."

9:00 a.m. - House of Representatives Chamber - Capitol Building

Fitzwilliams stepped into the chamber at 9:00 a.m. sharp. After yesterday's event, the House was full and buzzing with excitement. Fitzwilliams hammered the House into session and immediately recognized the Senior Representative from Massachusetts.

Martha Woodall stood up and calmly stated, "I would like to introduce an impeachment resolution against President Hawley and Vice President Harris for high crimes and misdemeanors."

The House fell completely silent.

Woodall continued: "My aides are now passing out folders with the evidence to support these charges. Please take your time to review."

Fitzwilliams: "I will give you an hour to review the documents, then we will reconvene for a vote."

As Fitzwilliams was finishing, Representative Jaden Sanchez, one of Hawley's closest supporters, stood up and demanded, "These charges need to be referred to the Judiciary Committee for proper investigation. You can't just railroad them through."

Woodall replied: "The membership can review the evidence; then we can decide in an hour if further investigation is needed. I take it, Mr. Sanchez, you don't own a TV."

9:30 a.m. - Speaker's Office - Capitol Building

Burr was already sitting in one of the side chairs when Fitzwilliams got back to his office. As Fitzwilliams was sitting down, Burr ventured, "Nicely done. I think you and Martha have things well under control. If you don't mind, I will take my leave for a bit but should be back for the final vote."

Fitzwilliams: "Thanks, Nate, I do think we have it under control."

Burr: "Just to help ground people, the fifty House members whose reelection campaigns received the donation the other night from President Washington will be receiving the following text message in about five minutes:

'All obstructions to the execution of the laws, all combinations and associations, under whatever plausible character, with the real design to direct, control, counteract, or awe the regular deliberation and action of the constituted authorities, are destructive of this fundamental principle, and of fatal tendency.' G. Washington, Farewell Address."

Burr: "If nothing else it should help ground anyone who might be wavering."

Fitzwilliams: "You certainly don't mess around."

Burr: "This is too important to take any chances."

9:30 a.m. - Bell's Study - The Townhouse

Bell had been up for hours. The proof was provided by the half-dozen half-drunk cups of coffee scattered across the desk. He muttered to himself, as soon as this is over, we are getting a better coffee machine for both here and the Lodge.

The secure handset he had placed on the desk lit up in front of him. The display read "Taylor."

Bell: "Morning, General."

Taylor: "Morning, Harry. I just heard from the SOG Commander that they have Harris in custody. They are asking what we want done with him."

Bell: "Charles, here's the plan. Working backwards, I am sending an unmarked Gulfstream G800 to Gettysburg Regional Airport. It's fourteen miles away and the nearest one we can land a jet. The plane will arrive at 3:00 p.m. Have the SOG Team deliver Harris to the plane as soon as it touches down. He needs to be sedated and secured in the rear cabin.

"We are going to use Elle's ex, Jimmy Walsh, to get Hawley out. Elle will text him with instructions shortly before 3:00 p.m. By 3:10 p.m. Hawley will no longer be President, which gives us more scope to operate in case something goes terribly wrong.

"Basically, all we need the SOG Team to do is drop a bunch of tear gas canisters down into the main command area and simulate a full-on attack. Walsh will rush Hawley out of the bunker and tell him they are getting him to a secure aircraft to fly him out. Walsh will drive Hawley to the airport, get him on the plane, and then we can take it from there.

"The only complication I can foresee is if other members of Hawley's security detail come with them to the airport. If that happens, your men will need to deal with it on the tarmac. In terms of people in the bunker with Hawley, have your men release them after they have been disarmed. The only one I want held is Agent North. I have information that he's the one that sent the team to grab Rockefeller at Rockefeller Center the other night."

Taylor: "Harry, I think that will work. What happens if Walsh can't get Hawley out?"

Bell: "Then we go down to get him, and people likely will die. Just as an aside, you know my nephew is part of SOG."

Taylor: "I do, Harry. He was a Marine, so didn't serve under me. Fine young man. In fact, he was the one that captured Harris. While I have you on the line, reports from Texas, Louisiana, Mississippi, and Arkansas aren't good. The Guard is still occupying voting sites in all those states. I ordered them all back to base this morning and so far not a single unit has complied."

Bell: "I'm not surprised. Let's focus on Texas. Once they comply, the rest will fall into line."

Taylor: "This has the potential to get ugly. I know the Texas Guard's Commanding General. He's still fighting the Civil War in his head. Funny thing though, the guy grew up in California. Just don't remind him of that."

Bell: "Do what you need to do. Just don't start another Civil War."

Taylor: "I'll let you know how it goes."

The talking heads on the monitors in front of Bell started reporting on the impeachment proceedings. In the background, for the first time in days, electoral maps were reporting voting tallies as they were streaming in. On one screen he spotted former Atlanta Mayor Lynn Tyler being interviewed and on another network Hollywood actor George Damon was discussing the Electoral College.

Tracy Rockefeller's head peeked through the door. "Harry, do you have a minute?" she asked.

Bell: "Of course. Coffee?"

Rockefeller: "Already well caffeinated. How are things playing out?"

Bell: "So far so good. The team is in place at Raven Rock. Harris is already in our custody. Impeachment proceedings are underway. Clark has been handled and the two Justices taken care of."

Rockefeller: "What do you need from me?"

Bell: "We will need Elle's help in a few hours, and we will need to get you over to the Supreme Court by 4:00 p.m. Lockwood will meet you here and escort you and Elle over. Hoyt and Lockwood will then take you to the Capitol where you will be sworn in as Acting President, probably around 5:00 p.m. if all goes to plan."

Rockefeller: "What happens next?"

Bell: "We will all meet here tomorrow. Hoyt will join us. He will ask us if the threat is removed. We will vote on the question. After the vote, we will return power to the people and their government. The country will be yours to lead, as the Founding Fathers intended. Then we will fade back into the fog of history."

Rockefeller: "My shoulders already feel heavy. I hope I can call on you privately for guidance."

Bell: "As the CEO of one of America's largest banks, I am always available to help."

They both nodded and Rockefeller understood.

10:00 a.m. - House of Representatives Chamber - Capitol Building

Fitzwilliams hammered the House back into session and immediately recognized the Senior Representative from Massachusetts.

Martha Woodall stood up and asked, "You have all now had time to review the evidence, and we have all lived through the events of the last several days. Does any member of the House believe these charges need further investigation?"

Silence. Representative Jaden Sanchez stared right at the floor.

Fitzwilliams: "Then I suggest we move to a final vote on the Articles of Impeachment against both President Edward Hawley and Vice President Joseph Harris. This will be a recorded vote so history will know how each member voted."

By 10:30 a.m. the final tally was in: Yeas 402, Nays 33.

Fitzwilliams: "The Ayes have it. Representative Woodall, would you please accompany me as we deliver the Articles of Impeachment to the Senate?"

10:45 a.m. - VIP Care Unit - Walter Reed Hospital

McCollins was resting quietly in his hospital room in the private VIP care unit. A TV silently reported on Hawley's impeachment in the background. His hand suddenly tightened; an alarm tone spiked as the monitor flatlined. Nurses flooded in and compressions started. Fifteen minutes later he was pronounced dead.

11:00 a.m. - Treasury Secretary's Office - Treasury Department

Burr strode directly into Cohen's office, right past the protesting executive assistant shouting that he needed an appointment and that Cohen was busy. As Burr walked into his office, Cohen held up his hand to his EA and motioned Burr over to his small conference table.

Cohen: "That was quite the power move and a bit risky, marching in here unannounced and without an appointment."

Burr: "I didn't think you would have agreed to see me on short notice, so I didn't risk the ask."

Cohen: "You are probably right, but since you're here, what can I do for you?"

Burr: "Bell sent me. The discussion you had yesterday on Mount Vernon LLC—that never happened, and Mount Vernon does not exist. Any trace of it in your system needs to disappear."

Cohen: "And what happens if it doesn't?"

Burr: "Well, you wouldn't be the first Treasury Secretary someone in my family shot."

Cohen: "That's clear."

Burr: "And you might want to turn on your TV."

11:00 a.m. - Base Commander's Office - Norfolk Naval Station

Taylor was operating on a limited amount of sleep and a maximum amount of coffee. He was very much looking forward to when this would all be behind him. What was now in front of him though was every commander's worst nightmare: American troops in a potentially hostile posture. This hadn't happened since the Civil War.

Taylor turned to his chief of staff. "Get me General Wells, Texas National Guard."

"Yes, sir," the aide replied, followed a second later by, "Sir, I have General Wells for you on line one."

Taylor: "General Wells, this is General Charles Taylor, Commander of USNORTHCOM. As the President has federalized the National Guard, you now report to me. I am ordering you and all your troops to return to base immediately."

Wells: "General Taylor, I report to the Governor of Texas and we are carrying out his lawful orders."

Taylor: "General, you and your men are in clear violation of §§ 592 and 593. If they withdraw and return to base immediately, I will order JAG not to prosecute."

Wells: "This is Texas and I will not be intimidated."

Taylor: "General, President Hoover said, 'Older men declare war. But it is youth that must fight and die.' I do not want to see young men going home in caskets today to prove an old man's folly. We all swore allegiance to the same flag."

Wells: "Your forces are hundreds of miles away."

Taylor: "My capabilities are on your doorstep. Take a look at the F-4 Phantom mounted right by Camp Mabry's main gate."

As Wells turned his chair to look at the relic from the Vietnam War, a Hellfire missile launched from a drone circling far overhead obliterated it. The explosion shook the entire base and splashed coffee all over Wells' desk.

Taylor: "General, have I made myself clear? You have fifteen minutes to get your troops moving. There will not be a second call."

1:00 p.m. - Senate Chamber - Capitol Building

The President pro tempore gaveled the Senate into session. The Vice President's chair on the dais was noticeably empty. However, the magnitude of the task they were about to be asked to undertake was made clear by the presence of Chief Justice Anthony Hoyt on the podium.

The President pro tempore rose from his seat, raised his right hand, and began the swearing-in process. One by one, each Senator rose and repeated the promise to do impartial justice according to the Constitution and laws.

Once the swearing-in process had been completed, Hoyt signaled Fitzwilliams and Woodall, acting as the House Impeachment Managers, to begin. Fitzwilliams rose and read the Articles of Impeachment that had been passed by the House that morning.

Clark then stepped forward and submitted that he was acting as representative and counsel for both the President and Vice President. Hoyt then nodded to Fitzwilliams to begin his opening statement.

Fitzwilliams: "In The Federalist Papers, Alexander Hamilton said, 'The greatest danger to republics and the liberties of the people comes from political opportunists who begin as demagogues and end as tyrants, and the people who are encouraged to follow them.' The framers of our Constitution understood that the greatest danger our nation would face was during an election, when the opportunities to interfere with both the vote and peaceful transfer of power would be most tempting.

"To quote Founding Father William Davie of North Carolina, impeachment is a necessary tool; otherwise, a president may spare no effort or means whatever to get himself reelected. Or as James Madison put it during the Constitutional Convention when arguing for the impeachment mechanism, it is for defending the community against the incapacity, negligence, or perfidy of the chief magistrate.

"The folders on the desks in front of you contain irrefutable evidence that President Hawley and Vice President Harris have committed high crimes and misdemeanors against the United States and its Constitution."

Silence filled the chamber. After a minute to let the gravity of the situation settle, Hoyt indicated to Clark to deliver his opening remarks.

Clark, gripping the podium with both hands:

Clark: "Mr. Chief Justice"—then turning to face the President pro tempore—"Mr. President, Honorable Senators, we do not dispute the facts as they have been presented."

Hoyt: "Noted. Do you have anything further to add?"

Clark: "We do not."

Clark then sat back down, sheet white and barely able to disguise his trembling. Audible gasps filled the chamber.

Webster then stood and was recognized by Hoyt.

Webster: "I offer that we should move directly to disposition."

One by one the Senators stood and voted. By 2:00 p.m. Hawley and Harris had been removed from office by a vote of 85 Yeas and 15 Nays. As soon as that vote was finished, Webster put forward a motion for a second vote on permanently banning both from ever holding elective office again. That passed by an identical margin.

Hoyt then rose, announced both verdicts, thanked the Senators for doing their duty, and immediately left the chamber and headed back to the Supreme Court.

Webster then stood and requested the President pro tempore to bring the Senate back into session at 4:00 p.m.

With that, the Senators filed out, with Webster and Fitzwilliams heading back to Fitzwilliams' office.

Clark, now humbled, publicly humiliated, his world shattered, left the Capitol silently through a side door and took a taxi back to his office.

2:30 p.m. - Speaker's Office - Capitol Building

Burr was waiting for them in the anteroom.

The television on the wall displayed a split screen of both FOX and ABC reporting on the latest election results. Results from Texas, Louisiana, Mississippi, North Dakota, South Dakota, Idaho, Wyoming, and Arkansas were starting to pour in. The boards showed Rockefeller at 252 electoral votes with Hawley at 47. It was shaping up to be a landslide.

The three filed into Fitzwilliams' office and Burr quietly closed the door behind them.

Burr: "Now the goal is to make sure you don't become our next President."

Fitzwilliams: "How?"

Burr: "Under the 25th Amendment, Congress is authorized to provide for a line of succession beyond the Vice President. Under the current Presidential Succession Act, with Harris now removed, you would become Acting President. However, the key words are 'Congress is authorized.' Call the House back into session and pass a one-time revision to the Succession Act making Tracy Rockefeller the Acting President until her full term begins on January 20th."

Fitzwilliams: "Given her commanding lead, I doubt we will have much pushback."

Burr: "Let's try to get it through the House at 3:00 p.m. and then bring it across to the Senate for ratification at 4:00 p.m. Fitzwilliams, you can then sign it into law. It will be your one act as temporary Acting President. I will then tee up Hoyt to administer the oath at 5:00 p.m."

Webster: "You sure you haven't done this before?"

Burr: "Fortunately not. But while I am thinking of it, as soon as Rockefeller is sworn in, I will need you to return that old piece of parchment Bell gave you the other evening."

Webster tapped his suit jacket pocket. "It's right here, Nate. It's never left my sight."

2:30 p.m. - Bell's Study - The Townhouse

Bell and the two Rockefellers gathered in the lounge. Sunlight streamed through the windows while the tinted glass prevented anyone from peering in. The monitors in the background showed Rockefeller at 252 electoral votes with Hawley at 47.

Bell: "Give it another hour and you should be the President-elect. Congratulations, Madam President."

Tracy Rockefeller: "Appreciated, but we are not there yet."

Bell, turning to Elle: "Do you know if Jimmy uses Signal?"

Elle: "They all do."

Bell: "Great. Send him the following and set it to disappear ten seconds after he opens the message:

'At 1510 a SOG Team will simulate an attack on Raven Rock with smoke and tear gas. Evac Hawley out of the northeast entrance; SUV will be waiting. Proceed to Gettysburg Regional Airport. Distance is fourteen miles and roads will be clear. Unmarked G800 will meet you at the airport. If Hawley asks, Harris arranged it with Hogg's help. Message will delete in 10 and your signal will be cut.'"

Elle: "Done, sent."

Bell picked up his secure handset and dialed Teruel. "John, have your people cut Walsh's cell now."

Bell then followed with a text message to Damon: "Please ask your wife's uncle if we can use RAF Northolt to refuel the G800. Make sure he is aware it is completely off the books."

2:30 p.m. - Command Center - Raven Rock

Walsh's cell vibrated once, indicating the incoming message. He pulled it out of his pocket, tapped the alert, and read it quickly. As he was putting it back into his pocket, North walked by and stopped behind him.

North: "Walsh, did I hear your cell ping? Do you have a signal? Let me see it."

Walsh nervously pulled his cell phone back out of his pocket and handed it to North. North tapped the screen. It was blank, and the upper right-hand icon indicated no signal. He tossed it back to Walsh.

3:00 p.m. - House of Representatives Chamber - Capitol Building

Fitzwilliams had ordered a number of monitors brought into the House chamber, which were now streaming the latest election results. The atmosphere inside was electric. As he hammered the chamber back into session, FOX called the election for Tracy Rockefeller as she crossed the winning threshold of 270. The screen reported Rockefeller 277, Hawley 111. The final tally would be even more lopsided.

Fitzwilliams recognized the Senior Representative from Massachusetts.

Martha Woodall stood up and stated, "Under the 25th Amendment, Congress is authorized to provide for a line of succession beyond the Vice President. Given the extraordinary circumstances we have all lived through over the past several days, and the fact that Tracy Rockefeller will become our next President, I would like to propose a one-time revision to the Presidential Succession Act that bestows upon Tracy Rockefeller the title of Acting President until her full term begins on January 20th."

Fitzwilliams: "I am in full support of this revision and move that we go immediately to a recorded vote so history will know how each member voted."

By 3:15 p.m. the final tally was in: Yeas 434, Nays 1.

3:10 p.m. - Raven Rock

The sirens started wailing, catching everyone by surprise. A second later, smoke and tear gas canisters came tumbling down air shafts. A voice from down a hallway screamed, "We are under attack!"

Walsh grabbed the gas mask from under his desk and put it on. As he was turning to get up, North grabbed his shoulder and yelled, "Where's the President?" Walsh signaled to the Presidential Quarters, and the two sprinted down the hallway.

As they neared the door to the Presidential Suite, the door opened and a confused Hawley stepped into the hallway. As North pulled a gas mask over Hawley's face, Walsh grabbed his shoulder and pointed in the opposite direction from where they had come.

The three then sprinted down the north corridor, up the escape stairwell, before emerging out into the fading light and damp gray November mist. Several Secret Service SUVs were parked under a carport on the left. Walsh pointed to the first and they ran to the car, sounds of gunfire in the background.

Moving first, Walsh took the driver's seat, with North and Hawley climbing in the back. Once in, North pushed Hawley to the floor and signaled to stay down. Walsh hit the start button and had the black armored SUV up to 100 miles an hour before they even hit Route 16.

Once clear, North pulled off his gas mask and yelled at Walsh, "Where is emergency evac?"

Walsh replied, "Gettysburg Regional Airport. VP Harris said yesterday he has a plane there on standby."

North just grunted in reply.

Walsh did the fourteen-mile run to the airport in under ten minutes. As he approached the airfield, he could see the Gulfstream G800 idling on the taxiway, front stairway down. A lone guard sat in the security hut with the barrier down, stop sign hanging innocently in the middle.

As Walsh turned onto the airport access road, he kept his foot pinned to the floor. In seconds the barrier was scrap wood, and the guard was covered in his afternoon cup of coffee.

Walsh wasted no time and steered the SUV right up alongside the staircase. They could see the pilots in the cockpit, but no one was standing in the plane door.

Walsh turned around and, using hand signals, indicated he would go up first and make sure it was clear. While North and Hawley stayed low in the back of the SUV, Walsh ran up the stairway and into the cabin, looking to the right as he entered.

The door to the rear passenger section was closed and the front was empty. As he turned to look to the left, the door to the crew compartment opened slightly and an older gentleman gave him the OK thumbs-up signal and pointed toward the SUV. Walsh instantly understood and, without missing a beat, swung back around and gave North the all-clear signal.

North opened the SUV door and pushed Hawley out first, pointing him toward the plane stairway. Hawley, confused and unsteady on his feet, staggered over and grabbed the handrail, pulling himself forward one step at a time.

As he neared the top of the stairway, Walsh reached out, grabbing him and pulling him into the cabin. As he did that, a lone shot rang out and North, who was two steps behind Hawley, crumpled to the ground, a small hole above his right ear.

As soon as the shot was fired, Walsh swung the door up and the pilots started taxiing. The SOG sniper disappeared back into the forest.

As Walsh turned around, a confused, panicked Hawley—sitting in the front right-hand side captain's chair—yelled, "What the hell just happened?"

Before Walsh could answer, the older gentleman stepped out of the crew compartment and tossed Hawley a bottle of water, saying, "Hydrate. We have a long flight."

He then turned to Walsh and said, "You must be Jimmy. Very well done. I'm John Teruel. I am a friend of Elle's."

Hawley, confused and shaking, never heard the aide come up behind him. There was a prick on his neck as the needle went in, then Hawley's world went black.

As Hawley slumped forward, Teruel turned to Walsh and said, "He will be out a few hours. We will be refueling at Northolt, and we will drop you off there. I've arranged private transport for you back from Northolt. There are plenty of snacks in the front; it's a long flight, so make yourself comfortable."

Walsh grabbed a bottle of water and a couple of granola bars before sitting down across the aisle from the comatose Hawley, his head completely spinning.

4:00 p.m. - Senate Chamber - Capitol Building

By the time the President pro tempore gaveled the Senate into session, all the major networks were reporting a Rockefeller victory by a landslide. They now had Rockefeller projected to win 373 electoral votes to 165 for Hawley.

With the outcome of the election now a foregone conclusion, the one-time revision to the Presidential Succession Act sailed through the Senate and was approved by a unanimous voice vote.

4:00 p.m. - Attorney General's Office - Department of Justice

Clark sat slumped in his office chair. He hadn't bothered to turn on the lights. The only illumination came from the last rays of the sinking sun falling through the windows. His tie was askew and his face wrenched with anguish. He was completely unable to process how, in the last eight hours, his life had become completely ruined.

He flipped the picture of his wife down onto the desk, unable to look at it. Memories of his father telling him he would amount to nothing after he got caught cheating in law school echoed through his head. While his father's money had eventually made that go away, the shame and insecurity had continued to haunt Clark.

After ten more minutes of just staring into space, he spun his chair around and opened the small safe on the wall behind him. Clark took a leather-wrapped package out and placed it on his desk. Slowly he unwrapped the package, revealing a German Luger pistol his great-grandfather had liberated from a German officer at the end of World War II.

He checked the magazine quickly; it was full. Clark shoved the pistol into his rear waistband and left the office.

4:30 p.m. - Bell's Study - The Townhouse

With Hawley and Harris now well out over the Atlantic, there was one more loose end to tie up at Raven Rock. He picked up the handset and dialed Taylor.

Bell: "Charles, it looks like it's all coming together nicely. I have one more favor to ask of the SOG Team at Raven Rock."

Taylor: "I just heard from the Commander, all is quiet on site. They think everyone is out. Most have been put on buses and sent back to D.C."

Bell: "Please have them sweep the bunker. Once they are sure it's clear, have them blow Hawley and Harris' suites out from the inside. The explosion needs to be large enough, so it's felt by the surrounding community. We will get the media to report it with the presumption that Hawley or Harris triggered the explosion to avoid facing justice. No one saw either leave the bunker, so it should hold."

Taylor: "With pleasure."

5:00 p.m. - Rotunda - Capitol Building

Chief Justice Hoyt and the two Rockefellers arrived at the Capitol right at 5:00 p.m. A small crowd had gathered and started clapping as Tracy Rockefeller stepped out of the black SUV. Rockefeller was dressed in an elegant navy blue suit, and Elle followed in a simple long dark gray dress. Hoyt was in his Chief Justice's robe.

The Secret Service immediately surrounded them as they proceeded up the left-hand staircase into the Capitol Building. Fitzwilliams and Webster, along with the majority of the House and Senate, met them at the top of the stairs.

As they stopped at the top to turn and wave to the crowd, Rockefeller signaled Webster to come over. As he did, Rockefeller took his hand and said, "John, I would like you to be my Vice President."

Webster smiled. "It would be an honor, ma'am."

The Rockefellers and Hoyt then headed inside to the Rotunda and beelined toward the statue of George Washington. For both Tracy and Hoyt, this was the perfect spot to administer the oath of office.

Elle pulled an old family Bible out of her purse and held it out in front of her mother. Hoyt then began administering the oath, with Tracy repeating the words after him:

"I do solemnly swear that I will faithfully execute the Office of President of the United States, and will, to the best of my ability, preserve, protect, and defend the Constitution of the United States."

As Hoyt reached out to shake Rockefeller's hand, a Secret Service agent on the far-right-hand side yelled, "Gun!"

Clark had entered the Capitol via one of the private side entrances and used his standing as a Cabinet Secretary to circumvent the metal detectors. When the crowd had started to fill the

Rotunda, he took a position quietly in the back on the right-hand side where he had a clear view of Tracy Rockefeller.

When she said, "Constitution of the United States," he reached back under both his overcoat and suit jacket and brought the Luger forward and up. As the barrel of the gun came horizontal, Clark pulled the trigger, firing the notoriously temperamental gun for the first time in half a century.

It was the last thing he ever did. As the Luger's trigger clicked, a shot directly to his left rang out. The 9mm round from the Glock smacked Clark squarely in the side of his head. The Luger fell out of his hand and, as it hit the marble floor, a shot rang out. The bullet hit the statue of President James Garfield, marking the second time the poor man was shot.

At "Gun!" the Rockefellers and Hoyt suddenly discovered what life is like as an NFL quarterback when the pocket collapses. Buried under a pile of Secret Service bodies, they slowly began to pick themselves back up after the "all clear" signal was given.

The group was hustled out of the Rotunda and went to the Speaker's office. The agent in charge finally asked if the now President was ready to go to the White House.

Tracy responded, "Tomorrow. Let's give the staff time to move Hawley's things out. I can stay at Trowbridge House tonight. Any idea who the shooter was?"

Agent: "It was Attorney General Clark. The gun he used was likely a World War II era German Luger as it had an Iron Cross embedded in the grip. Probably taken off a German officer at the end of the war. We are lucky Clark didn't know much about guns, the Luger's were known to be finicky and the bullets he had in were likely decades old. Even the German army stopped issuing them in 1939.

7:00 p.m. - Bell's Study - The Townhouse

The wall of screens in the study was playing back footage of the inauguration alongside reports of a massive explosion at the secret Raven Rock bunker.

Bell picked up the secure handset and sent a text message to all:

"Townhouse, tomorrow 5:00 p.m. Those of you who have Decrees, please bring them with you. Burr, please collect the one we gave to Webster."

Day 7 – The Sun Rises Again
Morning - Lounge - The Townhouse

The sun was just starting to peek through the curtains in the townhouse. The flickering light of three large, muted monitors danced off the walls in the lounge. A fresh carafe of coffee and a tray of cups sat on the sideboard.

Bell was sunk into one end of the large leather sofa, comfortably leaning against a pillow wedged up against the couch's arm. Burr reclined in one of the vintage Eames Chairs that were spread on either side of the coffee table. Between them, on the coffee table, lay an array of remotes. Bell grabbed one and started cycling through the different feeds starting with CNN. The headline read

ASSASSINATION ATTEMPT ON ACTING PRESIDENT ROCKEFELLER —
ATTORNEY GENERAL MARK CLARK DEAD

Grainy cell phone footage from the Rotunda filled the screen. The camera shook as someone shouted "Gun!" Agents lunged. A single muffled crack. Then the frozen frame of a dark-suited figure sprawled on the marble, a pistol skittered out of reach, the new President and Chief Justice buried under a pile of bodies.

The anchor's voice rolled over the images. "—Secret Service sources say the Attorney General, Mark Clark, drew a weapon as President Tracy Rockefeller completed the oath of office. An agent in the crowd standing near to Clark saw him draw the gun and fired, killing

Clark instantly. Acting President Rockefeller was unharmed. Clark's motives at this time are unknown. He did not leave any final notes or a testament.

Burr exhaled slowly. "That was too close for comfort. I really should have had someone keep eyes on him."

Bell: "I don't think either of us suspected he would snap."

Bell jabbed at the remote again.

FOX showed a live shot of the North Portico. The sun was just burning through the November haze, painting white columns in a golden hue. The headline read:

ACTING PRESIDENT ROCKEFELLER ARRIVES AT WHITE HOUSE

Rockefeller, looking elegant in an understated Chanel suit, stepped out of the armored SUV, flanked by Elle and a wedge of Secret Service Agents. They were taking no risks after yesterday's failed attempt. She paused at the base of the short steps, turning to wave at the small crowd on Pennsylvania Avenue that had gathered, pressing up against the fence.

The morning anchor intoned: "This is Tracy Rockefeller's first time arriving at the North Portico as the Acting President of the United States. We were told that in a private exchange just before taking the oath of office yesterday, Rockefeller asked Senate Majority Leader John Webster to serve as her Vice President. The White House has now confirmed she intends to formally nominate Webster later this week."

Bell looked at Burr: "Your suggestion?"

Burr: "I think it's a very good call, but my fingerprints are not to be found on this one. Rockefeller made this call all on her own. Didn't even know it was coming."

Burr then picked up the remote and changed over to the ABC feed as the visual had caught his eye. ABC was showing an aerial shot from a helicopter circling the Raven Rock site. Smoke still curled up from several different spots in the mountain. Emergency vehicles ringed the mud and rain-soaked perimeter, yellow police tape visible everywhere.

EXPLOSION AT RAVEN ROCK BUNKER — FORMER PRESIDENT HAWLEY, FORMER VICE PRESIDENT HARRIS PRESUMED DEAD

A correspondent in a yellow parka shouted into his mic over the thump of rotors and the screeching of sirens: "Authorities are not releasing any information about what happened here at Raven Rock, which was the site of a secret Presidential Command bunker. Late yesterday afternoon there was a massive explosion here that appears to have originated inside the underground complex. Locals in nearby Gettysburg say their houses shook. What we do know is this is where former President Hawley and his key lieutenants have been located for the last several days and initial reports suggest that they both were still on site when the explosion happened. If so, they are now buried under thousands of tons of rock."

The camera cut to a retired general in a studio in New York earning his keep as a paid contributor: "If they were in their private quarters when the blast occurred, the odds of survival are effectively zero."

Bell watched the smoke still threading up from the mountain: "That has worked out well. Saves us having to produce a body."

Burr laughing: "We did give them a very large explosion."

Bell: "Any idea what happened to Bolton?"

Burr: "None, apparently, he hadn't been seen in the bunker for the last several days."

Bell: "I wouldn't be surprised if he never turns up."

Burr: "That's probably best for all of us. He had the morals of a hyena."

Bell clicked the remote again, moving over to the BBC World feed.

A clip rolled of the British prime minister at a podium outside the front door of Number 10.

PM Allsopp: "I spoke with Acting President Rockefeller earlier this morning to congratulate her on her being elected the next US President. I said I was looking forward to building our personal relationship and strengthening our two countries special relationship."

Bell muted the sound again.

Burr: "They have been helpful."

Bell: "The King is a good man. Their current Prime Minister…..well at least she can follow instructions and knows not to ask too many questions."

He clicked back to FOX. Yesterday's emergency joint session replayed in a smaller box while a talking head with hair far blonder than it should have been droned on.

Bell: "Our job is done. Threat is removed. The right person is in the White House. That is the remit."

Burr: "The world thinks the mad tyrant died in his cave, his evil henchman was killed by a white knight defending the new queen, and then the queen and her princess rode up Pennsylvania Avenue to the palace. As myths go, it's not bad."

Bell: "You should give up law and go write stories for Disney. We have a few loose ends to still tie up before we meet tonight. I've already taken the pressure off Hawley Oil, there's no need for a bunch of innocent people to lose their jobs. We do need to talk to Taylor about Bragg."

Burr says while pulling out one of the secure handsets: "I'll get him on the line."

Taylor: "Good Morning Gentlemen, it's a good day to be an American."

Bell: "It is General. I'm here with Nate, we are working on tying up the final pieces, one of which is Bragg."

Taylor: "I'd like to let him retire honorably at his full four-star rank. At the end of the day, he did do the right thing, and he has served his country well for over 40 years."

Burr: "I concur, you shouldn't judge a person by the worst day in their life, especially if it happened over 35 years ago. His record since has been one of honor."

Bell: "Then we are all in agreement. Charles, please give Bragg a call and press upon him that he needs to put in his retirement papers today while it's still our call. If he waits, he might not get the same outcome."

Taylor: "Consider it done. I will let you know if I get any push back, but I think he is going to be relieved."

Finally, Bell reached for the remote and killed the screens. The room fell into a quiet, soft light. "I'm going to go take a nap. It's going to be another long night."

Bell then got up to leave, leaving Burr starting to flip through a large stack of newspapers.

12:00 p.m. GMT - Approach to Diego Garcia - Indian Ocean

The Gulfstream G800 dropped through the rolling white clouds into the thin tropical haze. You could almost see the heat rising off the ocean's surface. Below, the atoll of Diego Garcia curved like a bent horseshoe around the lagoon. The twin runways, and several low-lying buildings on the western side. A single track road ran south to where a few more buildings hung on the thin coastline.

Inside the cabin, the air was cool and dry, only the spinning of the engines disturbed the peace.

Hawley was slumped in the forward right-hand captain's chair, jaw slack, a faint line of drool at the corner of his mouth. A faint bruise marked the side of his neck where the needle had gone in and an IV now protruded from his right arm. At some point during the trip, his clothes had been changed, and he was now wearing an orange jumpsuit with the number 1 on the back. His hands were loosely strapped to the armrests with soft cuffs more to keep them from flailing around should they hit turbulence than anything else.

Behind the closed door to the rear compartment, Joe Harris lay on a gurney bolted to the floor, IV taped to the back of his hand, chest rising and falling in slow, drugged rhythm. He had also been changed into an orange jumpsuit with the number 2 on the back. A loose blanket covered him.

John Teruel sat at the small conference table, seat belt buckled, glasses low on his nose as he flipped through a biography of Washington. He did not look like someone delivering fugitives to a black site. White hair, open-collar shirt, a faintly rumpled blazer. Teruel looked more like someone's kind old grandfather rather than a master of the universe.

The captain's voice came over the intercom.

"Mr. Teruel, we are on final approach. Ten minutes to wheels down."

Teruel closed the book, tucked it back into his leather briefcase, and stood, bracing himself on the overhead bin doors as the plane began to bank. He looked once at Hawley, then walked back to the rear door, opening it to check on Harris and the two aides riding in back.

"Ten minutes," he said softly. The aides nodded and Harris snored.

He reached into an overhead compartment and pulled down two canvas duffel bags. One for each man.

Out of the window, the ocean rushed up to meet them, then rubber met concrete.

12:20 p.m. GMT - Secure Hangar South End - Diego Garcia

Upon landing the G800 had taxied to a low, anonymous hangar at the far south end of the airfield. Inside, the far too bright fluorescent lights hummed, and a pair of light white Air Force SUVs idled by the back exit. Two men dressed in all black waited at the bottom of the stairs. The cockpit door opened and the pilot waited by the door. Teruel looked up at the pilot briefly and said, "two hours then we head back to DC."

Heat swamped the cabin the moment the door opened. Thick, humid, and nauseating, perfumed with aviation fuel. The two aides checked both the unwitting passengers. Harris remained firmly out cold. Hawley started stirring slightly, mouth beginning to move and eye lids fluttering. The aide pushed a bit more sedative through the IVs and Hawley fell back into his chair.

"Get a board for Hawley and strap him down," Teruel said quietly. "It will be the easiest way to move his rather rotund body."

Hawley was eased onto a stretcher, IV bottle dangling off the side. They carried him down the stairs. Harris stayed on the gurney; they rolled him straight down the aisle, through the galley and onto a portable lift.

No one saluted, in fact no one said much of anything. The men handling the stretchers worked with the impersonal competence of people moving fragile classified cargo. Teruel got in the passenger seat of the first car and the 2 aides hopped into the rear of the second. Once both men were loaded into the back of the SUVs—Hawley in the first, Harris in the second—the exit door opened just wide enough to let both SUVs stream through, then closed back up with an angry bang.

The convoy took the road south along the lagoon, then turned right down an unmarked dirt lane thick with palm trees on either side. A couple hundred yards down, a heavy steel gate greeted them, security cameras hovering above it. A drone came over the gate and hovered over the front hood with its camera pointed into the first SUV. After a minute it lifted off and the gate opened. From above, the compound would have looked like a row of small townhouses built back-to-back, six units in a neat block surrounded by a high white wall that forming a crescent that was anchored by the beach. From the road, there was nothing but a long, flat white brick wall that disappeared into the palm grove and a single heavy steel gate. What was invisible from ground level, was the security center and interrogation rooms buried below the buildings.

1:00 p.m. - Longwood Cells #1 - Diego Garcia

Teruel had named these the Longwood Cells after Napoleon's final residence on Saint Helena. From the ocean, they looked like mid-market timeshare condos that would be at home on the Florida Panhandle. From the front, it was just a long white 2 story wall with several steel doors embedded into the poured concrete.

The front door opened into a small foyer, once inside the foyer and with the door closed, a second door could be opened into a lounge with a sofa, an armchair, a coffee table, bookshelf loaded down with copies of the Federalist Papers, several biographies of George Washington, and one each on John Jay, Alexander Hamilton, and Thomas Jefferson. A television was mounted on the wall with the remote on the coffee table. A kitchenette gleamed along the far side—stainless steel sink, induction cooktop, fridge, cabinets stocked with plates and glasses.

Beyond that, a short hallway led to a bedroom with a queen size bed, wardrobe, and built-in desk. Off the hallway, a door opened onto a tiled bathroom with a walk-in shower.

There were no windows on the front or sides of the unit. The only natural light came from the back: a set of sliding glass doors opened onto a small walled courtyard—high concrete walls on three sides, a thin electrified steel wire matrix across the top that let in ample light while both preventing any ideas of escape and shielding the courtyard from the prying eyes of any satellites far above. The Indian Ocean could clearly be heard over the top of the wall. Cameras watched every move from dark domes throughout the units.

The aides laid Hawley on the bed, propped his head up on a pillow, and started the process of bringing him out of sedation. "He'll be awake in about 30 minutes," one of them said. "He'll be nauseous and disoriented. That's normal. He will need about a half hour after that before you can talk to him.

Teruel nodded acknowledgment, and said, "I will wait here with Hawley, please go get Harris settled in. After I'm done here, I will walk down and talk to him."

The door closed with a soft click. The six pin security lock automatically engaged.

Once the aides were out, Teruel pulled a black circular bracket out of the duffle bag he had brought from the plane. He walked over and placed it around Hawley's right ankle. As he pulled a pin out of the bottom, a blue light started blinking on top.

8:10 a.m. - Longwood Cells #6 - Diego Garcia

At the opposite end of the block, Unit 6 was a near-perfect mirror image of Unit 1: same layout, same furniture, same collection of books, and same walled courtyard.

Different occupant.

Harris's gurney was wheeled into the lounge. The two of the aides hoisted him up and onto the bed. In the orange jumpsuit he looked like a giant orange banana against the clean white sheets.

The aide adjusted his IV, checked his pupils, and made the same pronouncement. "Thirty minutes then he should start stirring. I guess we wait here until Teruel comes down.

Two men, two ends of the same luxury cell block, separated by four empty units of silence and concrete.

Neither knew the other was there and nor would they ever.

10:30 a.m. - Longwood Cells #1 - Diego Garcia

Hawley came back to consciousness slowly as if swimming through seaweed and ocean grass. As his eyes slowly started to open, the light hurt. He could hear water and the scent of the ocean filled his nostrils. Slowly things started to come into focus.

The ceiling above him was white and smooth, with a recessed light and a small metal dome next to it. What that was, he couldn't figure out. The bed under him soft and the air smelled salty.

His throat was dry. His mouth tasted like cotton and his head was throbbing.

He pushed himself up on his elbows. The room swam. He waited until it steadied, then swung his legs over the side of the bed. As he looked down, he saw the orange jumpsuit. Further confusion washed over him.

Hawley's memory started coming back in jumbled pieces.

Raven Rock. Sirens. Tear gas. North and Walsh pulling him out of the bunker. The race to the airfield. North falling backwards, then an old man on the plane. Blackness.

Then here, wherever here was.

Hawley looked up as he started to stand up. In the corner of the room sitting in a lounge chair was the old man from the plane. Hawley froze.

"You," he said. "The old man on the plane. You threw a bottle of water at me."

Teruel smiled politely. "Good afternoon, Mr. Hawley. How are you feeling?"

Hawley's temper returned in a rush. "Where the hell am I? What is this? Do you have any idea who you're dealing with? I'm the President of the United States."

"Yes, I do" Teruel said mildly with a tinge of amusement, "and you were the President of the United States…past tense."

Hawley snapped. "Where is my Secret Service detail? Give me a phone now."

"Or what?" Teruel asked, the confidence in the question taking the edge off Hawley's rage. "You'll have me arrested?"

"Please, sit," Teruel said, gesturing toward the sofa in the lounge.

Hawley glared at him.

Teruel let the silence linger. "You're dehydrated," he said. "Have some water. It will help take the edge off and steady your head. You were out for almost 12 hours."

As the powerlessness of his situation slowing sank in, Hawley shuffled over to the sofa. His hands shook more than he wanted to admit. He picked up one of the bottles of water off the side table and unscrewed the cap.

"So," Hawley said, what the fuck is going on?"

Teruel smiled like a man in complete control of his environment: "we are on a small island in the Indian Ocean, approximately a thousand miles from the nearest mainland. The waters around us are shark infested. The currents are swift and can carry you miles out to sea in a matter of minutes. There are no civilian air or sea routes within miles of the island and it is well shielded from satellites. This previously uninhabited island is under the joint jurisdiction of two allied nations and its only occupant is an air force base.

Hawley stared. "Diego Garcia," he said slowly, memory stirring from some old briefing. "We are on Diego Garcia."

"You can't do this," Hawley said. "I'm the—"

"You were," Teruel interrupted, still polite. "Yesterday afternoon, while you were in dozing on the plane, the House of Representatives impeached you. Then the Senate tried and convicted you, finally voting to bar you from office permanently. Tracy Rockefeller is now President, and she's not a big fan.

Hawley shook his head, "I have the right to due process, your sham impeachment will not stand. The people will not allow it."

"Actually, they have, and the majority seemed quite relieved to have you out," Teruel replied. "One other thing you should be aware of, the nation thinks you are dead."

Hawley leaned forward, hands clenching. "So, what is this? Where are my clothes? You think you can just make me disappear?"

Teruel stood up, almost feeling sad for Hawley and intoned, "To start with, it's your new forever home and you might say orange is the new black. We have in fact made you disappear since the nation thinks you are buried under thousands of tons of rock."

He stepped back toward the door, then paused turning: "You will not be mistreated here. You will have food, water, exercise, medical care, and plenty of time for quiet self-reflection. Meals will be delivered three times a day in the foyer. Once you hear the outer door close, you will be able to open the inner door and retrieve it. You might have noticed the black bracelet around your ankle (Hawley had not and suddenly looked down), that's to make sure you don't have any ideas of leaving us unexpectedly. Should you venture fifty yards from your new residence, a small explosive will detach your lower leg from the rest of your body. Our doctors have estimated that you will bleed out in less than five minutes. It would be a really, horrible, painful way to do."

"Who can I talk to?" Hawley demanded. "Surely we can come to some sort of agreement?"

"For now," Teruel said, "you will mostly talk to yourself. In terms of helping to pass the time, we have put together a small library for you."

Teruel gestured to the bookshelf. "Several biographies of George Washington, a copy of his Farewell Address, and, of course, The Federalist Papers. I think you will find number 10 of particular interest.

Hawley stared at the bookshelf, eyes burning with anger. "You expect me to read this?"

"You will certainly have time to get through them all," Teruel said. "I may be back from time to time to ask you a few questions."

As Teruel was opening the inner foyer leave, Hawley stood up for the first time, shaky on his feet and hissed: "Who are you people? Why not just kill me now and get it over with?"

Teruel turned his head slightly. Locking eyes with Hawley he replied. "To start, we aren't murderous thugs like you lot. Who we are is not any of your concern. Welcome to your new, forever, home Mr. Hawley."

Hawley lunged but was still unsteady on his feet. He stumbled and caught the arm of the sofa instead and collapsed backwards onto it.

The door closed. The lock clicked. Hawley picked up the TV remote and turned on the monitor. A talking head on CNN filled the screen under the headline:

EXPLOSION AT RAVEN ROCK BUNKER — FORMER PRESIDENT HAWLEY, FORMER VICE PRESIDENT HARRIS PRESUMED DEAD.

11:00 a.m. - Longwood Cells #6 - Diego Garcia,

Joe Harris woke up on his back, staring at a white ceiling, feeling certain, in that first disoriented moment, that he had died and was staring up into heaven.

His head pounded. His tongue felt as if it had been wrapped in wool. He tried to sit up and instantly felt nauseous. As he raised his head, he became vaguely aware of two individuals seated in the corner of the room, dressed in black, just staring back at him.

The individual on the left, raised his hand and said: "Have some water. It will help take the edge off and steady your head. You were out for over 12 hours."

Harris spotted the small black dome in the corner of the ceiling. A small red eye stared back at him from within the dome. At this point he was thoroughly confused.

Harris looked at the individual who had spoken to him, "Who are you, where am I, why am I in an orange jumpsuit?"

The individual replied quietly, "all in due course. The boss will be along shortly to talk to you." The two men then got up and left, opening the door just as Teruel arrived.

The three men nodded to each other, and the second individual said, "He's awake, sitting up on the bed." Teruel said simply, "Good" and entered the foyer.

Teruel entered Harris' unit. Moving through quickly until he was standing in the bedroom doorway.

"Mr. Harris," Teruel said, voice courteous. "How are you feeling?"

Harris was thoroughly addled and confused at this point. Teruel's question went in one ear and out the other. Instead, he muttered: "Who are you? Where am I?"

"You are on an island in the Indian Ocean," Teruel said. "Roughly ten thousand miles from the nearest White House intern. Who I am is not relevant or important."

Harris swallowed. "I'm the Vice President of the United States, you can't do this to me."

"On the first, you were," Teruel said. "And on the second we have."

Harris gripped the back of the sofa. "There is no way President Hawley would allow this. If this is his idea of a prank, tell him I have plenty of dirt on him as well."

"You both no longer hold public office," Teruel said gently. "Yesterday, you were impeached, tried by the Senate, and convicted. Then you apparently died in a massive explosion at Raven Rock."

Harris's mouth opened and his eyes closed. He had never felt so helpless and confused in his life. Whoever this man standing in front of him was, he was more dangerous than anyone he had ever met. Desperate Harris finally asked, "Where is Hawley?"

"That's not relevant to your situation Mr. Harris," came the reply. "I've left you a few books to help pass the time." "Biographies of Washington. The Federalist Papers. A couple of volumes on the early Republic. And a Bible, I believe it's been quite a while since you actually read one."

Harris's shoulders sagged as the realization that he was now a prisoner finally fully settled in.

"How long?" Harris asked, voice thin. "How long are you going to keep me here?"

Teruel considered his reply for a moment, then said: "Since the citizens of the United States already believe you are dead, probably until that is a fact.....or you are no longer of use to us."

"But I've done nothing wrong," Harris protested.

"Grow up," Teruel replied, pulling another black ankle bracelet out of the bag. "Please put this on above your right ankle. It clicks into place. Once you have locked it, a small pin will pop out from the bottom. Please remove it and toss it over to me."

"Why the fuck should I do that for you?" replied Harris.

Teruel replied, "Look, we can do this the easy friendly way, or I can ask my two friends, who are standing outside right now, to come in and do it the hard way. They do have a bad habit of leaving bruises and really don't care for old men who prey on young women."

Without another word, Harris clipped the bracelet around his ankle and tossed Teruel the arming pin.

Teruel: "See, that was easy. Just in case you have any ideas about escape. That bracelet is programmed to explode if you leave this unit. If it does, you will bleed to death, in absolute agony, in a matter of minutes.

Teruel paused. The door closed. The lock engaged.

Harris sank onto the sofa, the surf's endless, indifferent rhythm beating faintly in the distance. His hands shook so badly he couldn't drink from the water glass.

Fifteen minutes later a Gulfstream G800 rolled down the runway and lifted into the cloudless blue sky.

5:00 p.m. - Boardroom - The Townhouse

The atmosphere in the townhouse's boardroom was significantly lighter this time.

The long table gleamed under the recessed lights, polished to a soft sheen. The portraits on the walls, Washington, Jay, and the original 13, watched, passing their silent judgment as always.

Outside the tall bulletproof and tinted windows, Washington, D.C., looked almost normal again. Traffic flowed, sirens screamed, and the sidewalks were full of footsteps. For the first time in days, all the monitors were off. Just a single large silver urn of fresh coffee sat on the sideboard.

Around the table, the Twelve of the Thirteen Guarantors sat in their accustomed seats. Only Rhode Island, John Teruel was missing. He was somewhere over the Atlantic by now, on his way back from Diego Garcia. At one end sat Chief Justice Anthony Hoyt in the old high-backed chair, a leather folio in front of him, glasses low on his nose. Bell sat at the other end of the table, the beech box on the polished surface before him, its lid closed, the faint impression of Washington's crest and Jay's scales still visible in the wax, now broken and flaked. One of the secure handsets lay next to the box. Bell picked it up and dialed Teruel in.

Hoyt cleared his throat while opening the folio. He lifted out an aged sheet of vellum and placed it carefully down in front of him. The ink was still dark, the handwriting unmistakable.

"My friends," Hoyt began, "the fifth rule under Washington's Decree is: remove the threat, then return power to its lawful channels at the earliest hour."

He looked up, eyes moving slowly around the table.

"The Decree gave us authority and power to act when certain conditions were met. It also binds us to stop when those conditions no longer exist. Washington and Jay were very clear on that point. The 13 are not, and never intended to be, a shadow government."

He put the vellum sheet back in the folio.

He straightened in his chair.

"As Chief Justice of the United States," he said, "charged under Washington's Decree to first invoke, and to then terminate the exercise of the powers granted by the decree, I put the question to the Thirteen Guarantors."

His gaze moved from face to face.

"Has the threat to the Constitution that justified activation of the Decree been removed and have the conditions been met so that power can be fully restored to the people's representatives?"

He gestured to Bell. "Per tradition, Harry will record the vote and affix his seal."

Bell pulled out a blank sheet of century old vellum.

One by one, the 13 answered.

"Massachusetts: Aye."

"Connecticut: Aye."

"New York: Aye."

"New Jersey: Aye."

"Pennsylvania: Aye."

"Delaware: Aye."

"Maryland: Aye."

"Virginia: Aye."

"North Carolina: Aye."

"South Carolina: Aye."

"Georgia: Aye."

"New Hampshire: Aye."

"Rhode Island: Aye."

Thirteen voices. Thirteen ayes.

Hoyt let the silence after the last one stretch for a moment. Then he nodded.

"The record will show," he said, "that by unanimous consent, the Guarantors find the threat removed and power is returned to the people's representatives." Bell then signed the vellum, folded it in thirds, affixed his seal and passed it up the table to Hoyt.

Bell then opened the beech box and removed six ancient documents. The original Decree, Washington's letter to the first among equals, and the letters to Commanding Officer, United States Army; Commanding Officer United States Navy; The Speaker of the House; President of the Senate. Bell then opened another small box to his left and pulled out a wax candle and an ancient seal. The seal was Washington's. With utmost care, he carefully resealed the documents one by one and then replaced them in the beech box.

When Bell was done, Hoyt stood up and said, "From the bottom of my heart, and on behalf of a grateful nation, thank you."

Bell then stood. "I would just like to thank you all. It's been a remarkable week. You have all made George and John proud. Meeting adjourned."

The remaining tension and formality in the room instantly dissolved.

North Carolina, George Damon, was the first to speak, "The world's watching, as always, and there is a palpable sense of relief across all of our friends."

Bell, his interest piqued, "You got a call?"

Damon smiled, and his eyes lit up. "Just before I came over," he said. "His Majesty sent his congratulations to President Rockefeller. This whole thing quite unsettled our friends across the Atlantic. A strong sane America is something they both count on, and value, extremely highly. As for telling off the Russians and the Chinese on our behalf, he quite enjoyed that part. My guess is that brought back fond memories of the Empire."

A ripple of tired laughter went around the table.

"Europe, Canada, Japan, Australia—everyone's lining up statements about the resilience of American democracy," Jackson added. "The markets like what they're hearing. Our allies are exhaling. Our adversaries are calculating what this all now means."

Bell had made his way down to the far end of the table and was standing next to Hoyt. He raised his voice slightly, "There is one small additional matter we need to undertake, later tonight, Anthony and I will return the box to Lawrence for safekeeping. Now may I propose a toast, to the "Great American Experiment", long may it prosper!"

With that, the 13 started to file out of the conference room. Hushed goodbyes and the gentle closing of doors followed. Within 15 minutes, the only two left in the conference room were Bell and Hoyt. "Harry," Hoyt said, "I believe it would be helpful to future generations to entrust a summary of this week's events to Lawrence's care." Anthony, Bell said, "I thought the same," as he pulled a separate folded packet, sealed with his initials, out of his breast pocket.

"Until we are needed again," he murmured. "God willing, not in our lifetimes."

11:30 p.m. The Old Tomb - Mount Vernon

Mount Vernon slept under a cloudy moonless sky.

The main mansion sat serenely above the Potomac, its white columns dark gray in the low light. The visitor center lights were long out; the last tour buses had rumbled away hours ago. Only the pale beam of a security car's headlights moved slowly along the perimeter roads.

Down the slope, past the smokehouse and the line of hollies that had watched generations go by, the Old Tomb crouched in its familiar hollow. Brick, iron, and earth. The little vault Washington had once called "unworthy," had helped preserve his "Great Experiment".

A dark SUV with DC Police plates rolled to a stop in the small gravel lot, lights off.

Hoyt and Bell got out without speaking.

They were dressed much as they had been on their first visit: Hoyt in his worn greatcoat and scarf, Bell in a salt-gray overcoat and an anonymous navy cap. The beech box cradled carefully in Bell's hands. Its value and power beyond calculation.

They walked the path from memory.

"Security?" Bell murmured as they approached the iron grate.

"Same as before," Hoyt said. "Four minutes after the hour, the guard pauses at the mansion to log. It's eleven twenty-eight now. We have a narrow window."

Bell pulled the odd, flat key from his pocket. The lock surrendered, just as it had before, with a weary sigh.

Inside, the air was cool and damp. The twin sarcophagus shapes in the back of the vault lay in their accustomed silence. The little rope in the corner hung silent.

Hoyt bowed his head slightly. "Good to see you again, Lawrence," he said softly. "We are returning a few of George's things."

Bell knelt by the loose brick near the floor. He eased it out, revealing the narrow cavity behind. The emptiness soon to be filled again.

"Boxes and a bell," he whispered.

Carefully, Bell slid the beech box, now wrapped again in oilcloth into the space until it nestled exactly as it had before, the fit perfect. The packet of modern notes went in beside it, wrapped in waxed paper against the damp.

He replaced the brick, felt it sit in place with a small, satisfying thunk.

Hoyt reached up and ran his fingers over the iron rosettes on the grate. The twelve stars in their eccentric pattern. One by one, he pressed them in the familiar sequence, feeling the hidden latch behind each reset.

Hoyt tugged the thin hemp rope in the corner.

Somewhere inside the brick wall, the tiny pewter bell chimed once, softly. The job now complete.

They stepped out and swung the grate shut. Bell turned the key in the ancient lock until it clicked back, sealing the entryway.

On the slope above, a flashlight beam swept once across the front of the mansion as the night guard made his rounds, then turned away. The Old Tomb lay in shadow again.

Back at the SUV, Bell slid behind the wheel but didn't start the engine. He looked through the windshield at the faint line of the river beyond the trees.

"You ever think Washington got it wrong?" Bell asked. "That maybe the true test of the experiment was letting it fail on its own terms instead of building a safety net only a handful of people know about?"

Hoyt thought for a moment. "He watched a king across the ocean go mad and drag a continent into war because no one could stop him," he said. "I think he'd have considered thirteen people with a conscience an acceptable hedge."

"And if, one day, they don't have one?" Bell asked.

"Then the experiment fails in a different way," Hoyt said. "But it is our, and our heirs, job to insure that doesn't happen."

"Do you think Rockefeller will try to drag us into the light?" Bell asked.

"And risk coming across as unhinged," Hoyt replied.

Bell laughed, then quietly said, "history will never tell our story."

Hoyt added, "and that's the way it should be."

Bell started the engine and slid a pair of night vision goggles over his eyes. Into the moonless night they slowly rolled.

The sun would rise again in a few hours.

The republic, bruised and shaken, would move forward again.

Washington's Decree slept again. With luck, it would never need to be invoked again.

Epilogue

On a brilliant, unseasonably warm, cloudless January 20, 2037, on the West Front of the Capitol, Tracy Rockefeller took the oath of office as President of the United States from Chief Justice Anthony Hoyt. The majority of the House and Senate were present, along with seven of the nine Justices and a carefully chosen scattering of figures from the worlds of art, business, entertainment, media, and sports. After the ceremony, during a brief meet-and-greet in the shadow of the inaugural platform, Harry Bell worked his way through the receiving line and reached Rockefeller just as she was speaking with Hoyt. He extended his hand, introduced himself to them both as the CEO of the Bank of Manhattan, and then, with a polite nod, moved on.

www.ingramcontent.com/pod-product-compliance
Lightning Source LLC
Chambersburg PA
CBHW022139240626
47153CB00007B/2420